CAN'T LET HER GO

GEORGIA LE CARRE

D1421942

ACKNOWLEDGMENTS

Many, many thanks for all your hard work and help,
Leanore Elliotte
Elizabeth Burns
Nichola Rhead
Teresa Banschbach
Tracy Gray
Brittany Urbaniak

Can't Let Her Go

ISBN 978-1-910575-89-5

KATYA

The old church is completely deserted. I huddle into my coat in the freezing air and slip into my usual middle pew. The wood is so cold it seeps right through my clothes and chills my skin. I try to close my eyes and pray, but it is impossible. My mind is full of a thousand whirling things.

"Hello, Katya."

Recognizing the voice, I snap my eyes open and get to my feet. "Good morning, Father."

The priest beams at me. "How are you, child? You will be leaving soon for America, won't you?"

I resist the urge to take a step back. I have never fully trusted him and tried my best to avoid him since he lifted me onto his lap when I was six years old and I felt something hard between his legs as he bounced me on his thighs. "In three days," I answered softly.

Father Georgiou nods. "You must be very proud of yourself. It is a great opportunity for you and a wonderful thing for your parents, not to mention for our village, and this blessed Church."

I bow my head in the customary gesture of respect. "Yes, Father."

He fingers the cross at the end of his rosary chain. "Well, tell your parents I might pop in tomorrow at teatime. I have a special treat for them. They deserve it. They are giving up their eldest daughter for the good of our community."

I smile politely. "Yes, Father."

"You won't forget us when you are in the land of milk and honey, will you?" he teases, a twinkle in his eye.

"Of course not," I say solemnly.

"Good." His face becomes suddenly grave. "Because your parents will be very sad if you do."

"I'll write back all the time and send money when I can."

He nods and looks pleased. "Good girl. I know you'll make us all proud." He takes a deep breath. "Right. I better be off. I need to prepare for my morning sermon tomorrow. Continue with your prayers, child, and I'll see you at your parents' house." He raises a playful eyebrow and waggles his index finger as if I'm going to turn eight and not eighteen in three days. "You never know there might be a little gift for you too."

"Thank you, Father."

The sound of Father Georgiou's hard, black shoes echo in the silent church as I sit down and bow my head. The sound stops when he passes into the inner chambers.

I bow my head and make another attempt at prayer. Of course, it is a great honor and a wonderful opportunity for me. I have been told many times that I should be grateful I'm good-looking enough to have been chosen to represent my village. Once I have done my duty, I will be offered a well-paying job. To that end, I have been taught to speak English from the time I was entered into this program.

But I can't help thinking that in three days, on Delivery day or D-day, I will be sent off to America as if I'm no more than high-end, carefully cultivated livestock. Like one of those Japanese black cows that become Kobe beef. No one will say it out loud, but that is exactly what I am. Raised to fulfill a rich man's desire. The only thing anyone in the village knows about him is his first name. Anakin.

It's been like that for almost forty years in my village. A girl on her eighteenth birthday is given away every five years. During other years, girls from other villages fill in the gap. I'll be the eighth girl from Sutgot.

When I was twelve years old my parents sent pictures of me, and to their delight I was accepted into the program. Since then, they have been getting a monthly stipend which is supposed to continue for the next ten years and from that day onwards, not a day has passed when they've not reminded me of my obligation to remain pure and unsullied. My entire value is based on that.

I tell myself I should be happy because I am helping my parents. If not for me, it would be very hard for them. They are hoping to move away from Sutgot. They want to go to the coast where it's warmer. My father is already thinking of sending my sister's photo when she turns twelve.

There is a shuffling sound behind me and I look around to see someone else has entered the church.

Mrs. Komarov nods at me and goes to light a candle. She is wearing the standard kerchief around her head, but hers is silk. I suppose she can afford it since it was her daughter who had her D-day five years ago.

I shut my eyes and give prayer one last chance, but my mind simply isn't here. I don't think God is listening to my prayers, anyway. If He were, there would be no delivery day for me. Eventually, I slip out of my pew and head for the exit.

To my surprise, I find Mrs. Komarov waiting just inside the exit. She looks anxious and frightened. "Katya," she begins, a tremor in her voice, "I feel I need to warn you."

I feel the hairs at the back of my neck rise. "Warn me?"

"Five years ago, it was my Saskia that went away. She was a good girl, a very good girl. In all the five years, I've never once heard from her. She was not that kind of girl. She would not forget her family. She would let us know she's alive. We raised her better than that."

I swallow the fear. "Do you mean to say you don't know what happened to her?"

"I spoke to the parents of the girls from the other villages and they have *all* never heard from their daughters once they go, even though they are all not bad girls who would never forget their mothers." She glances around nervously. "You must be careful. You must be on guard. The truth is no one knows what really happens to our girls once they leave Sutgot." Mrs. Komarov glances over her shoulder as if someone might be listening. She grabs my hand and squeezes hard. "You must not forget your mother and your father. You must let them know you're all right. And if you meet my Saskia, you must tell your parents, so they can tell me. Please, please, please, promise me, you will do this."

She is so desperate and half-crazy with fear I can't help pitying her. "I promise," I tell her. "I promise to let my parents know. And if I find Saskia, I'll make sure you find out."

There are tears in her eyes, and she opens her mouth, but can't find any words to say. Suddenly, she pulls me close and kisses my forehead. She smells of lavender powder. Her body is trembling and I get the feeling she thinks she's sending me to my death. In her mind D-day isn't Delivery-day, it's Death-day.

Then she crosses herself and hurries out the door.

I stand frozen to the spot, staring at her. If all those parents didn't hear from their daughters, that means—that means— it's not all sugar and happiness on the other side. I knew Mrs. Komarov's daughter. A good girl. Why in the world wouldn't she write to her mother? It didn't make any sense at all.

My knees are shaking as I walk home. I dare not even—I should talk to my parents. That is what I should do, but they already have the money from the program, and they are expecting more.

Oh, God—what is going to happen to me?

KATYA

My parents smile as I enter the house. My mother is embroidering a tablecloth and father is watching TV. His cheeks are already rosy with vodka. I know exactly what my parents expect. To hand over a virgin girl who is as innocent as a newborn. I'm a virgin, but I'm not innocent.

I know about sex, well, about how sex should work, anyway. I've watched a couple of old German blue movies with Russian subtitles. My friends tell me that real sex isn't like that. They say real sex doesn't involve guys with giant penises and girls whose eyes roll back in their heads as they climax.

In fact, my best friend, Irina says she has heard the whole act from start to finish only lasts about five minutes. It is wet and horrible, and the girl who told her about it said it didn't do anything for her. She'd rather bake a cake. I don't know about that, though. My body ached after I watched that first movie about the plumber and the housewife in the little apron.

"Father Georgiou said he might pop in tomorrow at teatime," I announce to my parents.

My mother beams with pride and pleasure. She considers it a blessing when the priest comes to our home. "Oh, good. I'll make his favorite biscuit for him."

"Mama, can I talk to you?"

"Of course you can. What is it, dear?" she asks kindly.

"Can we talk in the kitchen, please?"

My father turns his head back to the television.

My mother gives me an odd look. "Of course." She carefully sticks her needle into the cloth and gets up.

I lead the way to our little kitchen. There is a big pot of *Solyanka* on the stove and the kitchen is full of the warm, comforting smell of beef stewing in sweet sour broth. I turn around to face my mother.

"What is it?" she asks.

"Mrs. Komarov approached me at the church."

My mother sniffs. "What did that old gossip want?"

"She wanted to tell me that her daughter has never written to her ever since she left," I whisper.

"Hardly surprising. She's probably having such a good time in America, she has no time for that wet blanket and her constant grumbling and her—"

"Mama," I interrupt fiercely, "she said she had spoken to the other families who had joined the program and *none* of them has ever heard back from their girls."

My mother frowns. "What are you saying?"

I shake my head. "Something is wrong. Why would none of the other girls contact their families to say they are all right? I don't think we should continue with the program, Mama."

My mother closes the door. For a moment, she stands very still facing the closed door, her shoulders bowed. Then she walks to a wooden chair and sits down.

I stare at her as she gazes at the floor. The seconds tick by, neither of us speaks. The only noise is the muted sound of the television in the front room and the bubbling of the *Solyanka.*

Then Mama lifts her head and looks me directly in the eye. "I don't believe that woman. I have always thought she is a mean-spirited, jealous, malicious liar. She doesn't want our family to have the wealth that her family has received, that she enjoys until today. If it is true that she believes something bad has happened to her daughter and there is something sinister about this program that the Church supports why does she not go to the police? I'll tell you why. She doesn't because then …" She lifts her right hand and rubs the tip of her thumb against the rest of fingertips. "The lovely money will stop."

"But Mama—"

Mama shows me her palm. "I'm not finished."

I snap my mouth closed.

"She may think I am stupid, but I am not. I know exactly why she made up this story. She poured poison into your ear less than a week before you leave because she was trying to scare you. She was hoping you will bring shame and dishonor to our family by reneging on our promise. But she won't succeed. Her daughter is an ungrateful brat who took the first opportunity to abandon her parents. We raised you better than that. You are a good daughter. You will not forget or forsake your old parents, will you?"

I swallow hard and drop my eyes. "No, of course not."

"Good. Then we will talk no more about this. We will not give her the satisfaction of knowing you believed her even for a second. We gave our word and we have been living on the money from the program ever since. There is no way to back out of it." She stands, walks over to the stove, and starts to stir the pot of food. "You might as well go and fetch your sister and brother from the park. Lunch is almost ready."

Like a wooden puppet, I walk to the back door and open it. A blast of freezing wind tugs at the scarf around my head. I quickly pull the hood of my coat over my hair and close the door. In the distance, I can see my brother and sister playing with their makeshift sleigh.

My mind whirls as I start trundling through the thick snow towards them. There is a tight ball of tension in my stomach. I know Mama really believes Mrs. Komarov is a liar, but I saw something in Mrs. Komarov's eyes. I know she wasn't lying. Something is wrong. I know now that I can no longer rely on my parents. They refuse to see what is as plain as the noses on their faces.

My sister, Tatyana, is the first one to spot me. "Katya is back," she shouts and starts running towards me.

I watch her run, her face wreathed in a big grin. As she gets closer, I see how rosy her cheeks are from playing in the snow. It hits me like a speeding truck. In another year, she will be twelve and my parents will be enrolling her into the program.

She reaches me breathless and panting. "What's the matter with you? You look like you ate a bear's ass."

"Ugh … don't talk like that. If Mama hears she will be furious."

"Mama is not here, is she?" she counters cheekily. "Anyway, why do you look so upset? Is it because you will be leaving in a few days and you're going to miss me much too much?"

I pretend to grin. "Yeah, that's exactly it. Mama wants both of you to come in for lunch."

"Oi, Butt Head," she screams at my brother. "It's feeding time!"

HUNTER

Eddie-the-mooch stumbles out of O'Malley's tavern and because he is drunk, he doesn't see me. That's good because I don't feel like running him down. Not that I couldn't. He's a little fast, but he's no match for me, especially when he is drunk. He shuffles off toward his home, which happens to be an upstairs room in his sister's house. If I were her, I'd kick him out and count myself better off. She must have a soft spot for the little weasel.

It takes me twenty seconds to catch up with him and grab his arm. I make like I'm helping him stay upright, but I'm really keeping him from making off like a track star. "Eddie, what a coincidence. Good to see you."

He glances at me, and the blood runs from his face. He knows what this is about. Weasels always know when the fox has them cornered. "Hunter, hey, Hunter," he says. "Great to see you, great. How's it going?"

"It's going great for me," I reply. "But I'm not so sure about you."

He blinks as if he doesn't know what I'm talking about. That's one thing about weasels, they can put on the right face no matter what.

"Don't go soft on me," I tell him. "If you can't figure it out, that will just make things harder for you."

His eyes bulge. "Harder, how?"

"Well, going back and explaining why I'm here, well, that could take a lot more time. The more time I have to spend, the less patient I become. When I'm in a real hurry, well, things sometimes get out of hand."

I can feel that Eddie is getting ready to bolt. He's searching for a way to distract me, just for a moment. If he can lead me off the path for a moment, he'll take off. He doesn't care that I'll catch him. Desperation is starting to sober him up fast. It's a nice night. You couldn't tell it was already December.

"Hey," Eddie says. "You got a smoke?"

I give Eddie exactly what he wants. I let go of his arm. Eddie is candy.

He doesn't get a single step before I trip him. He hits the concrete hard. Before he can scramble to his feet, I kick him in the side. Not too hard. Not hard enough to crack a rib or bust up a spleen. Just enough to take out his wind. He lies on the sidewalk and gasps for air. I stand over him and light a cigarette. That's how you treat weasels.

You take away their hope.

"Eddie," I begin. "This is a nice night, a great night. I imagine there are a lot of women down by the bar, wearing tight dresses, drinking cocktails, and looking to get lucky. I wish I was with them. But I'm not and I kinda resent that. I mean, this is too good a night to waste on you, if you catch my drift. So, the way I see it, you got a choice. You can work with me, or you can go through thirty minutes of hell before you work with me. If I were you, I'd work with me and avoid the thirty minutes of hell. But, like I said, you got a choice."

He looks up at me, and I know the weasel has figured it out. At least, I think so until he rolls to his side to puke into the gutter. If he had thrown up on my shoes I would have had to really hurt him.

When he finishes, he rolls on his back and wipes his lips on his sleeve. I could tell him that he stinks, but I don't want him to think he has a weapon of some sort. Weasels will use anything they can find.

"That was a lot of good beer wasted," Eddie rasps.

"Knowing you, the beer was bought by everyone else in O'Malley's. So, you didn't lose nothing."

He laughs, and the laugh is cut short, probably because it hurts his throat. "You're right," he says. "The good paddies at O'Malley's don't mind paying for a good joke and a friendly smile."

"If you're thinking of making this thing last until you can try another run, you're making a huge mistake. I'll kick you every time you can take a deep breath."

"All right, all right, I hear ya, I hear ya. You're here about the money."

"It's always about the money. I'm a collector, Eddie. You pay me, or I hurt you. I'm sure you understand that."

"Yeah, yeah, and I'm sure you already know that I don't have the money. I mean, if I did, don't you think I would give it to you?"

I already know that the mooch doesn't have it. I knew that when he walked out of O'Malley's, but in my job, it's important that the guy admits he doesn't have the money. He has to know why he's going to get hurt. That way, he won't come back with a shotgun like he would if he thought the punishment was unmerited.

I drag smoke into my lungs. "How much you got?"

"Come on, Hunter, I don't have it all."

"How much, mooch, and don't make me go through your pockets."

"Three hundred."

"Let's see it."

He pulls off his left shoe and shakes out two hundreds. Then, he rifles through his pockets and adds five twenties.

"I don't get paid for a week," he says. "Can you leave me something for my sis?"

I pick up the money and drop two twenties on the sidewalk.

"Thanks," he says, "thanks."

"Here's the deal," I say. "I'm supposed to break your elbow if you don't have all the money."

"Aw, Hunter," he bleats. "You don't have to do that."

"I know, but it's sorta like my job."

"But if you do that," he wheedles. "I won't be working for a while, and it would be tough for you to collect anything from me next week."

I pick up the money. "Here's the deal. I'm not going to break your elbow. Stand up."

He struggles to his feet.

"I'm going to break your rib," I tell him.

"Aw … come on, Hunter. You know I'm good for it. You don't have to do that."

"Hold still, or I might puncture a lung." I grab his shoulder. "This will hurt, and it will remind you every time you breathe that I'm serious. Because next week, I expect the normal payment, plus what's behind. You got that?"

"I don't make that much."

"Yeah, you do, Eddie. You just got to stay out of O'Malley's for a week or two," I suggest helpfully.

"You think I can stay home with my sis? I don't go out, and all I hear is how effing lazy I am, how stupid. She drives me crazy. She's the one with the kid she can't afford, not me. And I'm the stupid one, right?"

"Take a deep breath and then let it all out," I tell him.

"Aw … please, Hunter."

I feel him take the breath and let it out. I hit him. Hard. I hear the rib crack, just like it's supposed to. He's skinny, so I only have to hit him once.

"What the …" he manages to rasp out.

15

"Yeah, it hurts, and it's gonna hurt. Maybe it will help you stay away from the beer." I pat him on the shoulder. "Look at it this way. You could have had a broken elbow. That would be a huge hospital bill and no work. Think how sis would rag on you then."

"You're a barrel of laughs, Hunter, a barrel of laughs."

"Last thing, mooch. Don't tell anyone that I did this to you. I don't want anyone telling me I can't hurt them real bad because I didn't hurt you."

He grasps his side dramatically. "I won't act the maggot, Hunter. Ya have my word."

Stop acting the maggot. The words flash into my brain together with the image of a young woman with curly dark brown locks and bright blue eyes. She is addressing the man whose shoulders I'm sitting on. We are on a beach running towards the water. I am clutching the man's head and laughing. We are all happy. I know instinctively this man and woman are my parents. Then the image goes as quickly as it had come.

I turn away from Eddie and walk away. The memory had only come because of unusual phrasing of Eddie's words. I push the memories away into that dark place where old memories live. I don't need the past.

The past can go to hell.

I fling away the cigarette and stuff the money into my pocket. Anakin won't be happy with me. He wanted Eddie punished. Anakin doesn't give a damn whether Eddie will be able to work or not. He believes every situation is an exercise in setting an example.

You don't pay, you get hurt ... bad.

Back in my tiny home, I put Eddie's cash in an envelope, write the name, the amount, and the date on it. Then I pull out the stack of envelopes inside my safe and chuck everything into a big leather knapsack. In an hour's time I have to deliver everything to T-Man, whose job it is to launder the money.

HUNTER

I deliver my stash of envelopes to T-Man. His office is in an old warehouse that Anakin owns. I hang around while he counts the money. His fingers are nimble and in no time, he is reaching for an envelope which he fills with my cut from the collections I've made.

Anakin is fair about that. If you collect, you get a cut. It's an incentive. The more you collect, the more you earn. I'm not sure he believes in capitalism or fair competition, but he understands bonuses.

Without exchanging a single word with him, I take my money and head across town to my meeting with Anakin. With Anakin, you bring in the goods before you go to talk. He is too smart to handle the money himself. If the Feds appear, he can claim he didn't know a thing. You can't label Anakin as an idiot.

Anakin's office is behind his bar. At this time of day, the bar is closed—at least to the public. The enforcers, like me, have no problem getting past Ruffie, the huge bouncer at the door.

Ruffie is the kind of guy that you never want to meet in an alley. Unless you're packing an elephant gun, you won't stop him before he reaches you. If he grabs you, he'll snap your neck in an instant. If I had to handle Ruffie, I'd do it with cleverness, not brute force.

I open the door and step inside.

Anakin is a Russian's Russian. He's big, bearded, and speaks in short bursts of guttural sounds. You're never going to read Anakin's expressionless face. He'll shake your hand as he shoves the shiv into your gut. "Hunter, Hunter, sit down, sit down," he says, with uncharacteristic expansiveness.

I sit because A) everyone does what Anakin wants and B) I'm curious why he is in such a good mood.

"Drink?" he asks.

"No thanks." I know I am not meant to accept. Not that I would want to. Who sits down to drink with a venomous serpent holding enough poison in its fangs to turn your blood into slimy tofu with one bite? Nah, I want to keep all my wits about me when I'm within spitting distance of him. Don't get me wrong. I don't hate him or anything. It is hard to describe my relationship with him. My parents sold me to him when I was four years old to settle their debt. Anakin brought me up. I remember my childhood as a time of unbelievable brutality and cruelty, but the suffering was sprinkled with flashes of kindness from him. A red, blue and white lollipop, a little pat on my head, words of praise, an encouraging gesture. They stood out. Making me long and crave for them. The mind games confused me so much, I mistook savagery for love and became like Pavlov's dog.

Ah, pain! Good. Kindness is in the horizon.

Years of Anakin's special brand of parenting and I learned absolute, total, complete loyalty to him. No matter what he asks me to do ... I do it without question. My allegiance is so blind I don't even think about the consequences of my own actions, the men I hurt, the long prison sentence waiting for me if I ever get caught for all those people I have planted into a bucket of cement and thrown off the pier.

"Did you break the Irish fool's elbow?" Anakin asks.

I know why he is asking about Eddie. People like Eddie are disgusting cockroaches to him and he wouldn't dream of wasting even a second enquiring about them, but once, a long time ago, I accidentally revealed a soft spot for their struggling souls and ever since, it has become his mission to crush that tiny bud of weakness inside me.

I'm twenty-four years old and my life is a meaningless, unfeeling journey of violence and depravity. This weak seedling of compassion is the only human emotion I have left and I'd let him snuff out my life rather than kill it. I shrug and keep my face expressionless. "I got as much from him as I could. If I'd broken his elbow, he wouldn't be able to work. If he can't work, he won't pay, and then, you're going to tell me to cap his knee." I shrug again.

Anakin's black eyes flash with irritation. "When will you understand the symbolic value of violence? Why do you think Mexicans carve off the faces of their enemies and lay it beside the corpse? You think they got nothing better to do?"

"Men like him never learn their lessons, so I'll probably have to put him in the ground inside six months, but today was not the day."

He studies me with that unreadable grin of his.

I don't know if he's going to pat me on the back, or stick his gun in my ear.

"You know, that's why I like you, Hunter. You think before you march to the music. I admire that. I can use that. I can give you a job and know you won't embarrass me. That's a good trait."

I nod because there is no telling if he's sincere, or setting me up for something really bad, but I suspect it's the latter.

"Your passport up to date?" he asks, changing the subject completely.

I don't know why he wants to know about my passport, but I'm not going to ask. "Yeah."

"Great, great, cause I got a collection for you."

"Collection?"

"In Russia. I got a package I want you to pick up."

What the hell is going on? I stare at him in astonishment. I already don't like the sound of this. "Like a Fedex package?"

He chuckles, but it's not a good chuckle. Russians don't do chuckles well. It's a guffaw, or nothing. "I like that," he says. "A Fedex package. No, it would be very hard to send this package by Fedex. I need you to pick it up. Ordinarily, I would send Anton, but as you know, he's up the river. He's … out of commission at the moment."

Anakin has a knack for killing off his darlings. You never want to be Anakin's darling. Anton never understood that simple lesson. I keep my voice light so he doesn't catch on. "I don't speak Russian," I lie.

"I never taught you Russian because I don't need you to know it. You will fly into Moscow and hook up with a guide. He'll handle all the talking. The package is ready to go. All you got to do is pick it up and not lose it. You do that, and you'll earn yourself a very nice bonus."

"Yeah, but …"

His face changes and I know I've said the wrong thing. He's picked me for this task and that's all there is to it. I don't get to pick and choose. "Hunter," he says very softly. With Anakin, the lower his voice becomes the more worried you should get. "This is a very important package, so important I'm willing to spend a lot of money to bring it back. I know you're thinking it's drugs, or some contraband that Customs will find and throw you into prison for a lifetime … or two. It ain't that way. The package is legit. I wouldn't lose you for anything. You're my boy. My best boy."

"All right. What is it?"

"You'll find out when you get there. Just follow the guide."

What is so important about this package that I have to fly half way around the world to get it? He's never even allowed me to leave America before. It doesn't make sense and perhaps that's the point. I'm not supposed to understand. I'm just the delivery man. Mr. UPS. To know more is to know too much.

"Your plane leaves in six hours and if I were you, I'd dress warm. It's always cold and unpredictable."

"Moscow?"

"Moscow is just the first stop. That's where you pick up your Sherpa and the train."

"I need a Sherpa?"

"In Russia, everyone needs a Sherpa, especially when you're looking at being on the train for three days."

"Three days?"

"First class, Hunter, first class." He says the words as if they're some kind of talisman, something that justifies everything else.

I don't need first class. I need someone to tell me the plan because it feels as if I've just stepped into the twilight zone. Anakin smiles again and it comes to me. I'm a sacrificial lamb. I wonder if he'll bother with a round-trip ticket because I don't expect to make it back. I cannot refuse my father. I have to go even if it means the end for me.

I don't have a choice.

I have to get on that plane and I have to meet my "Sherpa" in Moscow, and I have to catch a train (maybe). The train might be a mirage, something glimpsed just before you die of hypothermia on some barren wasteland in Russia.

I stand.

Anakin tilts his chin. His eyes drill into my being. "Hunter, the reason you are getting this job is because you are like a son to me. This is very important to me, really important. You do this right and you can rise in the organization. I need someone who has my back and will do the jobs no one else will do. And it's not just money. There will come a day when I won't be here and the next in line will take it over. That person could be you. Understand?"

I nod automatically, but I feel no pleasure or satisfaction. I know that this is the Russian mob. They're not going to let a guy named 'Hunter' take over. It's not in the cards, but I can't tell Anakin that. I have to let him think I'm gung-ho for this. In fact, I think it's a crock of whatever. I smile and nod and nod again. I'm the good soldier for my father.

On the way back to my apartment, I think of all the ways this trip to Russia can go wrong. I don't have enough fingers. This is the road to hell and I'm driving a fucking Ferrari at full speed down it.

KATYA

For two days, I worry about how I'm going to protect my sister. I know in my gut that if I am whisked away, never to be seen again, my parents will automatically assume I'm as ungrateful as Mrs. Komarov's daughter. Unperturbed, they will still sign my sister up for the program. I think about it constantly. And then it comes to me late at night as I lie in bed watching her sleep. Her face untroubled and innocent.

My real value to the program is my virginity. That's the requirement. All the girls have to be a virgin. We will be examined by a doctor in Moscow. What if I'm not a virgin? One little slip, and I wouldn't be one anymore. I'll be just another deflowered girl who isn't fit for D-day.

I consider my options.

Stay a virgin, get taken away and condemn my sister to the same fate. Or ... I could find a man to have sex with, which will disqualify me for the program. My mind starts whirling at the possibility and the consequences. I will be a fallen woman. The villagers will gossip about me. Obviously, my parents will be absolutely furious at the loss of face. My father may even disown me, but I will offer to take over the task of providing for our family. Then I will go to Moscow, work there and send money back.

But the true benefit will be enjoyed by my sister. Once I am kicked out of the program my family will no longer be trusted with the important task of providing another candidate to represent our village. My sister will be saved.

The only question becomes how to go about becoming a non-virgin. There are not a lot of options in my village, especially for a girl who has never even been on a date. Ever since my parents enrolled me in the program, they have protected me by keeping all the boys at bay. But I know there is a place where girls can 'hook up' with a man for temporary pleasure. The prospects won't be stellar, probably not even palatable, but I don't have many choices. Any man will do. I'll find someone. It can't be that hard.

This morning I go to see Irina and tell her what Mrs. Komarov told me.

Her eyes grow round as saucers. "What are you going to do?" she whispers.

"I'm going to lose my virginity," I whisper back.

Her mouth drops open. "What? You can't. What about your parents?"

"Yes, I can. My parents will get over it."

"Oh, my God. I can't believe this is happening. Are you sure?"

"Yes, I'm very sure. This is the only way to protect Tatyana."

"But no one has ever done such a thing."

"Well, then I'll be the first."

She frowns. "What about the money your parents have taken from the program?"

"I'll pay it all back, over time. I intend to go to Moscow and work there."

She scratches her head in bewilderment. "What will you do there?"

"I don't know. Anything. I could be a waitress or I could work in a kitchen. I don't care."

"Oh, Katya. Won't you think again? Moscow is such a dangerous place and you don't even know anyone there."

"My mind is made up. There's something wrong with the program, Irina. Even before Mrs. Komarov told me about the girls disappearing, I didn't feel good." I press my belly. "Here."

"How do you plan to lose your virginity then? Nobody in the village is going to sleep with you. They all know it's your D-day in four day's time."

"I'm not going to sleep with anyone from this village."

This time, Irina's eyes nearly pop out of her head. "What do you mean?"

"You know how your brother goes to Vatskoe every Friday night to have a drink ..."

"Yeah," she gasps in a hushed tone.

"I'll tell my parents I want to spend my second last night in Sutgot with you. I come here and hide in the back of his truck. Once we get to Vatskoe, I'll go to that tavern where all the truck drivers gather. I'll sleep with one of them and as soon as the act is over, I will hop back onto the back of the truck and wait for your brother. When we get back here, I'll wait for him to go into the house before I slip into your bedroom."

She gapes at me incredulously. "Are you crazy? Do you realize it's an hour's drive just to get there? You will freeze to death in that open truck."

"No, I won't. I'll bring my bear skin and hot water bottle."

She shakes her head in confusion. "But those men in the tavern. They're uncouth and dirty."

I feel a shiver go through me. Do I really want to do this? "It is just the one time. I will wash when I come back to your house."

"But what if you get pregnant?"

"That's what I'll need you for. Can you steal a condom from one of your brother's packets?"

"Me," she squeals. "Steal one of Yuri's condoms? Are you crazy?"

"Oh please, Irina. He'll never know. And even if he does realize one is missing and asks you, all you have to do is pretend it wasn't you. He'll think he made a mistake or dropped it. Please, Irina. This is really important."

"All right," she agrees reluctantly.

I lean forward and kiss her. "Thank you. Thank you so much! I won't forget this."

"I'm not happy about this. I think you're making a mistake."

"I know you do, but I'm doing this not just for myself but for Tatyana too."

"You do know your way around Vatskoe, don't you?"

"Like the back of my hand," I lie. I've been there once with Papa and his friend. I sat in the car while he and his friend went to get some specialty vodka for his daughter's engagement party.

HUNTER

Anakin was true to his word and I fly to Amsterdam first class. It makes me realize I'm not walking into a trap. He would never flush money down the train for a walking corpse. The attendants try to feed me every fifteen minutes and set down a new drink every ten. They're pretty too, and they smile as if they're interested in me. They aren't. And I'm okay with that. I know what I look like. I'm a big, ugly motherfucker with an angry scar down my face and dead eyes, but they're just trying to get through the time without making me unhappy.

In Amsterdam, I change planes and airlines.

While the first flight was all smiles and good reviews, the second flight is cold war all over again. The smiles are perfunctory; the booze is watered down; the food is left over from a prison riot or something. But I'm not complaining. I'm worrying about the package.

In Moscow, I exit customs after they have done their worst with my bag to find the Sherpa waiting. Sherpas come in various flavors and this one is old, way old, older than anyone in Anakin's organization. His dour face is lined and leathery as if he has lived on a mountain all his life.

He speaks English far better than I speak Russian, but he is a man of few words apparently. We head to the train station. Apparently, spending a night in Moscow isn't included in the itinerary. I look at the Sherpa as he makes his way to the platform and wonder if he's packing heat. I would feel better if he did, because I certainly don't want to carry a pistol in a foreign country. That's a recipe for prison. Russian prisons aren't known for their hospitality.

We board the train and find our first-class cabin. As first-class goes, it is about third class, but it is private and it is bug-free. Not that I'm one of those guys that hates bugs. When I was a kid, cockroaches were my bedmates. I hated them until I loved them. I used to share my food with them.

But that was a very, very long time ago.

As the train leaves the station, I catch glimpses of Moscow. A thought comes into my head. *One day I will be back here. Like a tourist. Like a normal person.* The thought surprises me. I never make plans for the future. The future is a black hole. I glance back at the Sherpa.

He is staring blankly out of the opposite window.

I turn away and do the same.

Train rides are inherently boring. No matter what you do, it's always more of the same. Some towns, some cities, lots of open country. The train isn't exactly a high-speed miracle. It goes faster at times and slower at times and then, it sits on a siding while another train ambles past.

The Sherpa speaks when it's time to eat or drink. He likes to drink, and apparently, he has a large expense account. When he says it's time, we saunter down to the bar car and start on the vodka. While I can generally hold my own with American Russians, I'm a piker compared to the Sherpa. He drains shot after shot, and it doesn't seem to affect him, although it must. Only a robot with a robotic liver can drink like this Sherpa. After a couple hours of vodka, we move to the dining car. The food is awful, so we don't eat much. The Sherpa drinks some more and I settle for vegetables and bread. It's good bread. The meat is a mystery, but it tastes like broiled beef. Maybe when we get to where we're going, I'll find a decent burger or something.

The days run together, the miles fall behind and I wonder again, why in the hell I have to travel all this way for a package. What really bothers me is that the package must be something incredibly valuable. Anakin is no idiot and he doesn't waste money. He's not going to send me halfway around the world for a box of Cheerios. Translated, that means I'm a target on the return trip. People are going to know I'm bringing home the crown jewels and every thief worth his salt will be looking to relieve me of my treasure. I don't like my chances.

After three days, we roll into a small town. The trains shudders to a stop at the station and the Sherpa grabs both bags.

"Have we arrived?"

He shakes his head. "No, this is Vatskoe. A storm has damaged the rail tracks up ahead. We will stay the night here and travel to Sutgot by car tomorrow."

I follow him to a small inn, the kind of place you would see in an old movie. A dour, middle-aged woman places large bowls of steaming potato and beef stew in front of us before showing us to our rooms.

My room is spotlessly clean, but smells like cabbage. It's a common smell. The train smelled like cabbage and the station smelled like cabbage. Hell, it feels as if everything and everyone in Russia smells like cabbage. As the sound of her hard shoes shuffle away on the wooden floor, I turn towards the small window. For a long time, I watch the snow falling outside. The sight is magical. Again, the thought comes into my head. I will come back to this beautiful country as a tourist.

Then I brush my teeth and without undressing, I climb between the freezing sheets. My body rocks on its own even without the train. Sleep doesn't come. I try to push thoughts of that damn package out of my head, but I can't. I keep thinking I'm a sitting duck out here. Finally, I give up and get out of bed. It is too early to be in bed, anyway.

Despite the freezing weather, I decide to explore the town.

KATYA

https://www.youtube.com/watch?v=ksdAs4LBRq8&
-just take me anywhere with you-

My parents don't smile when I tell them I'm spending the night with Irina. They're not happy, but they're not suspicious. It's not like I've painted my face or doused myself with perfume. They have no real clues to go on. It's just the second last night before D-day. They're anxious. The prize is so close. On the day of the exchange, they get an envelope full of cash.

The bear skin and hot water bottle are already at Irina's house and I feel calm as I hurry towards her house in my thick clothes. I know I do not look sexy, but I will put some red lipstick on later. My mother bought it for me. It was supposed to be worn on the night I lose my virginity and the irony is that is the way it has turned out even though it will not be to the man of my mother's dreams.

Everything goes to plan. Irina manages to steal a condom from her brother for me and by the time he comes out of the house after his meal, I am as snug as a bug inside my bearskin. It is dark and his truck is filled with building equipment that he uses for work so he doesn't notice me.

The ride is horribly bumpy and my body feels bruised when the truck comes to a stop more than an hour later. Yuri jumps out and is soon gone to the bar where all his friends meet every Friday. I peek out carefully. There aren't too many people around and good news … he has not parked too far away from the tavern.

I hop down to the ground, my boots sinking in the soft thick snow. First, I wrap my hot water bottle tightly inside the bear rug so it does not lose heat too quickly. Then I shrug off my coat, peel off the two layers of sweaters and the thick, ugly tights. There is so much adrenaline rushing through my veins I do not feel the cold even though I am standing in my blouse and skirt. Once I get my coat back on, I carefully apply the red lipstick, remove my head scarf, and smooth down my long honey blonde hair.

Squaring my shoulders, I take the first step towards the tavern.

Outside the door I hesitate, but only for a second, then my hand grasps the handle and I push open the door. It's a long bar down one side, filled with smoke and men who turn to stare at me. It's all about being macho, tough and drunk in here. I don't know all the problems that plague Russian men, but I know a few. They drink too much, work too little, pretend they're some kind of tough guy.

I look down the bar and there isn't a single man that appeals to me. But then, I don't need a man who appeals. I need a man who knows how to have sex. That's all and the faces staring at me seem to promise at least that much.

The other side of the bar is all booths, half-filled at this time of night. Couples occupy them. They're here for a few hours of fun. They throw darts, eat and drink, then maybe when they leave, they'll be happy enough to go to work in the morning, not that there are a lot of jobs in this part of Russia.

I wade through the smoke, looking for a place at the bar that isn't close to any of the men leering at me. A fear runs through me. This isn't my territory. I'm a fish out of water, but I'm not going back. If I lose my virginity, I won't be shipped out. If I lose my virginity, I won't go someplace where I can be raped or killed or whatever and no one will ever know. This way, it will be on my terms.

Before the barman can attend to me, a man in a leather jacket smiles on his way over. "You look thirsty. Can I buy you a drink?"

He could be the one. I nod. Instead of asking me what I want, he orders me a vodka, which is fine with me. I'll need more than one to have sex with him. I am conscious of every man in that bar staring at me. They're all thinking the same thing. I swallow hard. "Do you have a cigarette?" I ask.

He produces a cigarette and lights it for me. I have never really smoked, once or twice with my girlfriends, but I feel so naked, so exposed. He passes me the cigarette and my hand trembles as I take it from him. As my drink arrives, I tell myself that the whole act will take only minutes. Once it's done, I will not have to disappear like the others. For a while, my parents will hate me, but that would be better than disappearing into some old man's harem. That would be too awful and to have my innocent sweet sister join me there. It would be unbearable.

"I know who you are, you know," the man says.

I blow out smoke and watch him through the smoke. "Really?"

His eyes are full of curiosity. "Aren't you supposed to be leaving tomorrow?"

I feel sick. I wish I'd never asked for the cigarette, but it is too late now. I hold the cigarette far from my face. "Does everyone know about me?"

He shrugs. "Of course." A strange light comes into his eyes. "But the real question is what are *you* doing here?"

My drink arrives and I toss it down quickly.

The man takes the hint and orders me another. He recognizes my mood. He doesn't know what I'm looking for, but he knows I'm looking for something. He hopes I'm looking for him.

I'm not. I need a man who doesn't know who I am. A stranger who will disappear into the night forever. One, I will never need to come face to face with again.

Before the second drink arrives, the door opens and a man walks in. He is mysterious and magnetic in a way none of the local men are. Big and strong with a scar running down one side of his face. His eyes are sparkling blue, but ... dangerous. That's the only way I can describe those eyes, because they're looking right at me, turning my insides into liquid.

I don't lower my eyes because I find his eyes mesmerizing.

They draw me in. Where did he come from? He's not from here. None of the older men have faces like his. In fact, I'd lay a bet that he is not even Russian. He is a foreigner. A surge of unfamiliar heat rushes through me, and it isn't the vodka. He has that kind of energy.

He moves down the bar until he's standing next to me. The man who bought my drinks takes one look at the stranger and backs away. There is an animal thing about the man. He slaps money on the table. Far more than the drinks are worth. When the bartender arrives, he brings two vodkas, one for me and one for the stranger. Everyone in the bar understands. There might be a few men who would challenge the newcomer, but even those men don't stand a chance.

Then, I realize the truth.

This man is pure sex. He is the real thing. He makes the movie I watched about the plumber with the big penis and the housewife seem ridiculous now. All those close ups of their shiny private bits over her fake cries seem … plastic and shallow. This man standing next to me is raw and primal, the manifestation of sex, of joining, of using.

He is Adam, the first real man. He is it.

I don't have to look around to know that every woman in the room is lusting for him. There might even be a few men who would walk out the door with him. Yet, he isn't looking at them. He's looking at me. A shiver runs up my spine. I came here to break my hymen and I thought I would have to do it pushed up against a bathroom wall with a truck driver who hasn't washed for many days, instead I found … this wordless, clawing need to go with a man.

I want to be with him. I want to feel him. I want him to feel me.

I kill the cigarette in the ashtray and we toss down the drinks, I will leave with him. He will take my virginity, then I will stay with him for as long as he will have me. Why do I think that? Why do I want that? I can't answer my own questions. I have never felt like this before. I'm certain that I want to feel like this again. I want sex. I want him.

He seems to sense what I want, because his dangerously beautiful blue eyes never leave mine. "What is your name?" he asks in Russian.

This surprises me. I did not expect him to speak Russian. "My name is Katya," I say in English. I don't want our conversation to be heard by anyone else in the bar. Gossip travels fast in these parts.

He seems even more surprised than me. He didn't come to a tiny Russian town and expect to find a girl who speaks English. "Who else speaks English?" he asks in that strangely hypnotic voice of his.

"Probably no one else here."

"Are you with the man who was just here?"

"No."

His lips twist. "It's good to know I won't get a knife in my back."

I shrug. "I'd still not turn your back. In Russia, no one trusts no one. We are all in it for ourselves."

He nods slowly in understanding. I think maybe he knows all

about being in it for himself. Why do I think he might be mafia? He looks the part, dangerous, lethal.

"I'm at the only hotel in town," he says.

"Yes, I know."

His eyes darken. "Room eleven."

My heart is hammering away, but I try to keep my expression casual so that no one around us understands what is going on. "Hmm …"

"If you don't come, I'll understand," he murmurs. But I can tell he doesn't mean it. He knows I'll go. He knows I can't stay away even if I wanted to. He is the desire that cannot be resisted. I have never wanted to be with a man who was so sure of his own sexuality and power before. Now, I feel I might like it—if the man is him.

Everyone watches him leave. He walks out the way he walked in. It's as if he came only to see me, even if he couldn't know that I would be here. Of course, he didn't know. I got lucky. He just got lucky.

"Who was that?" the man who bought me the drink asks as he sidles up to me again.

"I don't know," I answer.

"But you talked to him. What did he want?" he asks belligerently now that the danger is past.

"I don't know. He didn't say. I think he just came in here to get a drink."

The man's face shows disbelief.

I stand.

"Are you leaving already?" he whines.

"Yes, I have a big day tomorrow."

"Do you want me to walk you out?"

I look him in the eye. "Thank you, but that will not be necessary. I belong to another man."

He nods quickly and looks awkward. For a moment there, he had forgotten I'm in the program.

Everyone in the place stares at me as I walk to the door. Let them stare. I don't care. Soon, I will be leaving for Moscow. I will never have to see any of them after tonight. The same goes for the stranger I'm going to meet at his hotel.

I have only about a couple of hours before I have to go back to Yuri's truck.

HUNTER

https://www.youtube.com/watch?v=bo_efYhYU2A

I pace my room restlessly. Picking up a young woman in a foreign country is as dumb as dumb can be, but I couldn't stop myself. She was impossible to resist. I walked into that dump of a bar and I couldn't believe my eyes. What would a woman like that be doing in a shitty town in the middle of nowhere?

She was like a dream. Those luscious red lips. Hell, I wanted to grab her, throw her over my shoulder and take her back to my hotel. I'm still haunted by those emerald green eyes fringed by thick lashes, the smell of her. Roses. I hear footsteps in the corridor and rush to open the door before she can knock it.

"Oh," she says and drops the hand she had raised.

Fuck, she looks even better than she did at the smoky bar. She's incredibly, unbearably, mind-blowingly sexy, and as I look at her, I feel my control starting to slip. Making me want to pounce on her like an animal.

She smiles.

I don't smile back. I can't. My skin feels tight and hot and my heightened senses make me feel almost dizzy. I don't want her to know just how much I desire her. I don't want to scare her away. Even I don't understand what's going on with me. "Come in," I tell her and step aside.

She walks in, and out of habit I check the hallway for other people. I'm used to all kinds of scams, but I cannot really believe this is a scam. I close and lock the door. The room is suddenly full of the smell of roses. After having cabbage in my nostrils for days, I inhale it in greedily.

She bites her juicy, wet bottom lip. "You have anything to drink?"

I want to suck that lip into my mouth, instead I shake my head. "Who's coming?"

Her enormous green eyes widen. "What?"

"Is it that guy you were talking to?" Words drop out of my mouth, but I'm on autopilot. Years of conditioning has taken over. What I really want to do is fuck. Mindlessly. For hours.

She frowns. "I don't know what you're talking about."

"I was born at night, just not last night. Young, sexy girl gives some chump from out of town the eye. They get naked and some thug comes through the door. The chump gets tossed and if he has enough money, he ends up with a busted nose and an empty wallet. I know couples in Detroit that make a living out of dumb tourists. So, who's coming?"

"You're stupid," she says scornfully. "Are all Americans as stupid as you?"

There's something sweet and innocent about her even when she's being sassy, and yet she can't be that innocent. She has come to the room of a man she met in a bar for a few seconds. "Who's coming?" I ask harshly.

Her eyes flash.

Oh, I like that. Fire in a girl turns me on like nothing else.

"No one is coming," she says hotly. "Can't you get that through your thick American head?"

"Sit down," I tell her in the coldest voice I can muster. "We're going to wait a minute or two. We're going to talk. If no one comes through that door, then, we'll get to what we both want. If someone is coming, you better get on your phone and tell him to call it off. Because if he comes in, I'm going to break both his arms, so he'll have to pay someone to wipe his ass. Got that?"

She glances at the cheap plastic watch on her wrist, then sits down to wait with me.

I can't even pretend to care anymore. I don't care who's coming through that door. My body aches for her. I can accept a broken nose for her. "What's your name?" I ask. I know she told me her name, but I was so entranced by her face it flew right over my head.

"Katya. What's yours?"

"Hunter."

"Hunter?" she echoes. "Like in hunting for animals?"

"Exactly like that. Tell me about your family. Any brothers or sisters?"

She frowns and I don't blame her either. This must be the worst fucking seduction in the history of mankind. "Why do you want to know?" she asks.

"I don't actually. I'm just making conversation." The words taste like ashes in my mouth. I do want to know about her. I want to know *everything* about her.

"Then we will wait for your imaginary assailant in silence." She unbuttons her coat. I know she isn't doing it to be provocative, but hell, I can feel my temperature rising. I want to rip off her clothes and feast on her. She discards the coat and I feel my body responding. I tell myself any man would respond to this. Her curves are the stuff of movies and romance book covers. Curves to die for.

"This is really boring." She pulls her blouse apart and she's wearing a lacy black bra.

I open my mouth and no words come out.

The sight of me gaping idiotically at her lush body emboldens her. She stands and takes off her blouse, then wiggles out of her skirt. It's been a long time since I saw a girl take off her clothes without turning it into a provocative striptease of some sort. She reaches behind her back, unhooks her bra and lets it fall to the ground. Her nipples are pink and erect. She stands in nothing but her panties.

She's precisely what I want. What I really, really want.

My cock is hard and pushing against my jeans.

Resting one hand on the arm of the chair she takes one boot then the other off. Straightening, she hooks her thumbs into the waistband of her panties and pulls them down.

I can't help it, my mouth makes a shape and a groan escapes from my throat. My mouth is dry as I look at the neat nest of dark blonde curls. Jesus Christ. "How old are you?" My voice is unnaturally husky.

"Old enough," she answers. Her smooth, pale skin holds a pink flush.

I can't stop looking at her. She is so damn beautiful. "How old?"

She looks at her watch. "Fifteen minutes ago, I turned eighteen."

Eighteen. It's been a long time since I've been with someone that young. Something about her bothers me and it's not her age. The way she stands there naked and silent. Any other woman would have gotten into some kind of seductive pose. I still can't get away from the feeling that she is ... "Are you ... a ... virgin?"

She smiles sweetly. "Try me and find out."

Her voice is playful and teasing, and it makes me feel silly for thinking something like that. Of course, she isn't. A virgin doesn't follow strangers from a bar back to their hotel rooms. Maybe all Russian girls took off their clothes to just stand there buck naked, unaware of their own desirability. I forget about someone breaking down the door.

"Get on your knees," I tell her, the words hard and commanding.

Her eyebrows rise in surprise, but she drops to her knees obediently.

"Now, crawl over here," I order. Part of me thinks it is sacrilegious to make those flawless knees scrape the ground, but I need her to. I have to diminish her in my mind. She isn't a beautiful angel who visited me one snowy night in Russia, she is just a woman I met in a bar who followed me to my hotel room. It's just sex. Nothing more. My life is in Detroit. This is just another one-night stand. I've had many of those.

She gets on all fours and crawls towards me like some kind of feral animal, untamed and dangerous, but I don't think she knows what dangerous is. I'm dangerous. She's just an incredible beauty. To think that such a woman could be in this sad excuse of a town is astonishing. Her movements are slow, sensual, and while she crawls, I undo my pants and pull out my cock. It's throbbing now. It's full and red, but she's going to give it great attention before I let it shoot. I don't touch it. I let her see it, red and engorged, staring at her.

She arrives, and her eyes focus on my erection. Her eyes grow big and sparkle when she sees how big I am. Her red lips glisten when she licks them. She's excited as I am for this.

"Get to it," I breathe.

For the first time since I met her she appears unsure of herself and hesitant, then she rises to her knees and places her hands on my knees. Her skin is wonderfully soft. Some part of my brain wonders how this could be. It's as if she doesn't work and from what I know of Russia, every woman works—unless she's from a rich family. Katya's not rich. I can see that much. She squeezes as she leans forward, her pink tongue slips through those red lips and finds the head of my cock. She licks quickly like she would an ice cream. Ah, she has no idea how to please a man.

HUNTER

https://www.youtube.com/watch?v=tt2k8PGm-
TI&index=9&
From Dusk To Dawn

"Y ou've never done this, have you?" I ask incredulously.

"Many times," she answers immediately.

"Don't lie. I liked it when you were brutally honest."

She bites her bottom lip and shakes her head.

A thunder crack of pure lust sets my body off. I can't even think past the roaring in my ears. "I'm going to teach you how to do it. Listen and learn."

She nods and she's so fucking sexy it hurts.

"Lick slowly, linger, taste it."

A shiver goes down her back and she obeys, licking slowly, methodically.

"Swirl your tongue around the head as if you're making love to it. Don't think of me, think of my cock, think about making it want you. If you please it, it will take good care of you."

Her wet pink tongue moves up then down and around my engorged flesh and … she gets it. She starts making love to my member. True, she came to it unskilled, but I have to give it to her. She is a quick learner. Impressively quick.

I need those juicy lips wrapped around my cock. "Suck it," I tell her.

Her pupils dilate as her pretty mouth stretches itself around the head, and my body starts to tremble. My hands claw into her soft hair. I don't know why I'm reacting to her like this. It's crazy. I've never been a man who allowed a woman, any woman, to lead me around by my dick.

"No teeth," I tell her. "Just keep doing what you were doing. I want to fill your belly with my cum."

She moans with excitement at the thought. I feel her warm tongue quiver along the underside of my cock as she sucks me. It is as if she is milking me. I close my eyes. I don't want it to be over so quickly, but I don't think I can hold out much longer.

It is a shock when the inexperienced siren suddenly sucks me to the back of her throat. The thick veins in my cock pulse as I look down at her. It is a beautiful sight to see her naked and on her knees sucking my reddened raw cock for all she's worth. She's truly got a mouth made for fucking.

Holding onto her head I start to thrust in and out of her mouth. She takes it like a champion. Shallow thrusts that slowly travel deeper and deeper into her hot mouth. I can feel her excitement as she sucks harder and deeper. She's turned on by blowing me. Knowing that almost pushes me over the edge.

"Fuck, Katya. Your mouth is too hot. Too good. I can't hold on. I'm going to come," I groan as I grip her head and explode in her mouth. I feel her swallow around the head of my dick as my cum shoots deep into her throat. She sucks up every last drop.

We lock eyes and I feel something. Something I've never felt before. A voice in my head says. *Katya, my Katya. Mine.* Jesus Christ. Where did that come from? I don't want to keep her. Besides being a stupid, utterly meritless idea, I just can't. There's no place for a beauty like her in my ugly life. One of these days, my life will be cut short with a bullet in my head. I won't do that to any woman. It must be because I am in a foreign land. I'm not myself.

This is just a one-night stand. After tonight, I will never see her again. The thought makes me feel strangely lost and bereft which in turn makes me angry with myself for being such a sap.

I reach down and grab her breast. It's round and perfect, firm, as only the very young can be. I run my thumb over her nipple, and she moans helplessly. A part of me wants to just throw her on the bed and take her, but I'm not going to do that—yet.

I want her to get so aroused she begs me to take her. I want her to feel as desperate for me as I do for a taste of her pussy.

She bobs up and down on my softening dick. I squeeze both her breasts and she moans louder.

"Crawl to the bed," I tell her, pulling her off my cock.

Looking up at me with those beautiful eyes, she wipes her mouth. Then she turns and crawls, not too fast. She must know how fucking good she looks from behind. I'm going to spend hours eating that sweet pussy. With my gaze on her bare ass, I strip.

She crawls onto the broken down bed and faces me. Her face shows that she likes what she sees.

I tell myself not to be a fool. Sure, some women go nuts for my brooding, don't-come-close energy, but my body is full of monstrous scars and ugly homemade tattoos. Hardly, a sight for sore eyes. I remind myself that she's a very young woman, but a woman nevertheless, and women are never transparent. They smile as they betray you. Anakin used to remind me to smile before I slid the knife between someone's ribs. He said a smile disarms your opponent. Frown or snarl, and the guy would be on guard. Smile, and you could kick him in the nuts. While Katya looks as innocent as a puppy, she's probably more like a cat mercenary and manipulative.

I stop at the edge of the bed. She looks so beautiful and fierce on the mattress, her hips wriggling with anticipation. All this time, I was starving for this and I didn't even know it. I feel as if I should kneel at her feet. I don't recognize myself anymore. Me, a killer, a monster wanting to fall at the feet of a young girl and serve her.

"You're a virgin," I say softly.

"Yes," she whispers. For a moment she is silent, then says, "I have a condom."

"You won't need it yet."

I grab her ankles. My hands look dark and rough against her creamy smooth skin. I spread her legs and her sweet innocent pussy opens up like a dewy flower waiting to be claimed. The hole is so fucking small it gives the impression it has never taken even a finger. As I gaze at it, nectar flows out of it and my mouth begins to water.

I drop her ankles and with my palms pressing on the insides of her thighs, she opens up like a butterfly. As I bend my head, I already smell the heady scent of her arousal. Quickly, I swipe the tip of my tongue down the sweet split of her sex and my mind explodes with how perfect this moment is. This is how it is always supposed to be.

Her breasts jiggle as she shudders with pleasure.

I stop to watch her.

No woman has reacted like that to such a simple gesture. It feels good to be the first man to taste her, and it will feel even better to be the first man to enter her and claim her.

Her fingers twist impatiently in my hair.

"You want more?"

"Yes, yes," she begs breathlessly.

"Be patient, baby. My tongue is going to want much more than one little swipe. I'm going to push apart your lips and go so deep inside you, you're going to have to bite the pillow to stop your screams."

She looks at me as if she thinks she's died and gone to heaven. She's not far wrong. I plan to satisfy her in every which way I can. With a growl, I surge forward, part her pussy with the tip of my tongue and drown in her smoky sweet taste.

"Oh God," she rasps.

I'm the first one to touch her there. Gently, I press my thumbs against the swollen soft flesh and expose her little white nub. With my tongue, I circle the shy bud while she whimpers and moans. The sounds fill my head and make me feel like an untamed beast taking his mate for the first time. Seed begins to fill my balls again and my dick stretches to its full length. I'm going to be first inside her virgin pussy. Her first dick is going to be an American one.

Her head turns from side to side as I pleasure her. When I plunge my tongue into her sweet hole, she screams and jerks on my hair. Unsure if I have hurt her I lift my head, but she pushes my head back down on her pussy, her open thighs wriggling and squirming.

She grinds her pussy on my tongue. "Don't stop. Please don't stop!"

I begin to suckle at the pink bud while her juices drip from my chin.

"Stop, stop, I think I'm dying," she shouts suddenly, but I refuse to stop. I know exactly what is happening to her. I slap a hand over her mouth and just carry on suckling her while her body buckles, bows, and contracts as her juices gush. When the spasms subside, I remove my palm.

She looks at me with wide eyes. "Is it like that every time?"

"It's never the same."

"Oh, wow! Are you still going to …?"

Fisting my hard, heavy dick, I rise up over her and fit on a condom I had left by the bedside table. Then I slide between her legs and position the thick mushroom head of my cock at her entrance. "Grab it and rub it on your pussy."

She obeys, rubbing the head up and down along her soaking wet pussy lips. I reach down and use my fingers to spread her lips. She takes the hint and rubs it deeper, getting my swollen head wet and ready. But she doesn't push it in. I know she doesn't know what to do, so I push deeper into her. She moans and arches her hips. I stroke slowly, opening her. She's tight, very tight and I know that if she is a virgin, I'll have to break through. I stroke, holding onto her hips, pushing, worming, making her feel all of it. It won't be as easy as it might be with an experienced woman, but then, an experienced woman wouldn't be so tight. I want this tightness. I want to stroke and work. The reward will be something I've never had before. I stroke a little faster, a little deeper, and I reach the point where I stop.

I look into her eyes. "You know what has to happen?" I ask.

"Yes, I must take you inside me."

"You sure you're ready?" I ask, although I'm not going to stop, not now.

"I am sure. Do it."

"It may hurt like crazy," I warn.

She grips the sides of my head, tugging me down. "Kiss me," she whispers, her voice shaking. "Can you kiss me, please?"

HUNTER

https://www.youtube.com/watch?v=SQTHB4jM-KQ
(Wild Horses)

I crush my lips to her as her arms wrap around me and her sweet, pliant mouth opens beneath mine, allowing my tongue to sweep inside. She meets the dance of my tongue … and bliss. Complete and utter bliss. I never thought I'd experience this in my life. It intoxicates me and I kiss her like a starving man. I don't take my lips away from hers even as we both fight to catch our breaths, inhaling and exhaling through each other's mouths, our chests rising and falling in rhythm. Her hips jerk under mine, inviting me to fuck while she sucks on my tongue.

But I'm not going to bust her open just yet. I don't want her to scream. I slip two fingers into her wet pussy. Fuck, but she is tight. Really tight. And I am really big. It's not going to go well for her. She looks into my eyes and I can see that she trusts me. She shouldn't. I'm doing this because she's just too sexy and too willing.

With my other hand, I caress her breast. I don't stop stroking. I'm trying my best to lull her into some kind of trance. If she's focused on something else, this may not hurt so much.

She moans and jerks her hips, telling me she wants it.

I know this is the moment. I pinch her nipple hard and her mouth opens in a gasp. While she is distracted with that sensation, I push my big ugly dick into her beautiful virgin cunt—in one smooth movement.

I feel the breakthrough and so can she. She doesn't scream, but her eyes pop wide open. I know I hurt her. I can feel that I hurt her.

She swallows hard.

"Are you all right?" I ask.

"Yessss," she whispers. "Finish. I want to feel you finish."

"Sure?"

"Sure."

I stay still and let her adjust, feel, accept the intrusion. She pants as her lips are pursed tight. I hold until her eyelids flutter. She's ready for me to stretch her again.

I start to make shallow thrusts. I'm so fucking aroused, I can hardly bear to keep making these shallow thrusts when all I want to do is ram in all the way.

"Go on. Go all the way," she urges.

I don't hesitate. I can't stop. I slam into her and I explode. Her eyes widen again, and I can tell she feels it. No, she's not having an orgasm. She'll have to wait for that. A better man than me will give her that. But I have an orgasm, a great orgasm. I hold her until I don't spurt any more. I'm panting. I'm sweating. Sex with Katya is consuming. I roll off her, my erection fading. She lies beside me. Her breathing is not as labored as mine. We don't touch. I don't think that's a good idea. I'm leaving in the morning as soon as the Sherpa and I collect the package.

At another time, in another place, I would work until she has an orgasm. She deserves that. But this is Russia and I'm some stupid American on a mission that I don't understand. I shouldn't have gone out and I shouldn't have had a drink, and I sure as hell shouldn't have picked up Katya. Now, I was in that predictable post-sex guilt. She deserves better. But I'm not going to tell her—as if she didn't already know. I can't tell her that I want her gone. I can't tell her that I probably won't remember her a year from now. I can't tell her that I'll make sure I don't remember her. It's just sex, just sex.

There are a lot of *I shouldn't haves* running through my mind.

She is mesmerizingly beautiful, but that isn't what transfixes my gaze to her as she lies sprawled by my side, her nipples swollen and reddened, perhaps by the ever-lingering ghost of cold air in the room or the fact that I had been unable to stop sucking on them. What glues my gaze to her is quite simply the fact I can't look away. I don't want her to catch me staring so greedily, but I just can't seem to drag my gaze away. I feel my chest warm up dangerously as I find myself pulling the sheet up to cover her in case she's cold.

I instantly stop myself. *What the fuck am I doing?*

I jerk the covering completely away from her to expose her pale lush breasts and pink nipples, perfectly rounded and perked to attention as though ready once again to surrender its owner completely to me.

"I must go now," she whispers.

"Not yet. I'm not finished."

"Only if you are quick or I will lose my ride back."

I cover one creamy mound with my mouth and suck viciously on its sweetness. She responds with a sharp intake of breath. I lift my gaze to meet her slightly widened eyes. It's a dare, but for what ... I don't know. I'm prepared to hold her down, to have my last feast of her before she goes away.

Her response is to arch her body into mine and claw her fingers into my hair. She is pure fire. It's almost hard to believe that a woman of such passion and heat was a virgin until a few minutes ago, but my thrust through the barrier of her sex and the visible stain of blood against the sheets couldn't be contested.

Her gaze slides down to my cock. It is already rock hard with bulging veins.

"Do you see how hard you make me?" I accuse.

A sweet smile of power spreads across her luscious lips and I feel it as a kick to the heart. I slam into her almost vengefully and her back arches off the bed.

The moan from her throat is deep. I keep my eyes glued to her face as I pull slowly out of her, watching as the grating of my dick up her tight textured walls has her breath coming in short, fleeting spurts.

Her eyes are clenched shut and I hate that.

She grabs my hips when I almost slip out of her, her eyes shooting open to meet mine in an almost threatening glare. She doesn't say a word but none is needed.

"Keep your eyes open," I growl.

Those green jewels stay on me as I slam my cock back into her. Her hands bundle the bedsheets beneath her into fists. *Fuck!"* she gasps, in Russian.

I feel a smile settle on my lips. Her soft, but fiery tone makes the curse sound like an enchantment. An invitation to sin. To fuck until the world outside dissolves again.

She releases the sheet and throws her arms around me, urging me on. I drive hard into her, her hips rising and gyrating to meet my thrusts down into her core, as she squeezes every ounce of pleasure out of me. I fuck us both senseless, my balls slamming hard against her as we damn near break that rickety bed.

She claws her nails down my back as she cries out words that are incoherent to me. All I can do is feel the storm of ecstasy that possesses my entire body and quickly leads me up to the edge of a cliff I very much want to jump off of.

As if she had read my mind she grabs my hips and urges me frantically on, pounding her soft pussy onto my shaft. I go with her. Submitting completely to her as she milks me of all that I am.

"Come with me," I snarl and at the command, she explodes. Her cries and my groans fill the small room, resounding off the walls and hitting our rutting bodies. I shoot my seed into the condom, hot and deep and never ending, as I feel her juices splashing on my thighs.

My hips refuse to stop, driving into her mercilessly until we both can't breathe. I collapse on top of her, my face buried in her neck in sheer wonder … and embarrassment. I had lost complete and utter control. What kind of bewitchment is this? For the first time in my life I lost control of myself. She holds onto me tightly as we slowly come back to earth and even when I try to pull out of her, as I become aware of the intimacy of our position she locks me in place with her legs curved around my body and refuses to let go.

I feel a strange reluctance to move too. This will be our last time and I don't want it to be. I want to keep her.

"We won't see each other again, but that's OK. I got what I wanted. I hope you did too," she murmurs in my ear.

I shut my eyes. Shit. This is my punishment for all the girls who wanted to make it more and I blanked them off. Now the shoe is on the other foot. Finally, I know how they felt. I try to tell myself she is just a one-night stand. That I can't get soppy over her. That she's just something that happened to me in the wastelands of Russia, but it all feels hollow and depressing. "I got the better," I answer. "But thanks. If I offer money, will that offend you?"

"Yes. I'm not a whore."

"I know, and I'm sorry.

Sometimes after sex with a woman, I'll leave a bill or two, something to help with the rent, but I can't even bring myself to do that.

I touch her cheek, and she smiles. She has a great smile.

Her beautiful eyes look sad suddenly. "I better go."

I move my body. It feels like lead.

She slides off the bed and starts to get dressed again.

I watch her blankly. She is leaving. I want to stop her, but something inside me won't allow it. I know I cannot have her. Even if I took her back to Detroit with me, Anakin would ruin it. The only time I felt something for a girl was when I was nineteen. Mary-Jane had just got off the bus from a small town in North Dakota when I smiled at her. She was so innocent and green she still had hay in her hair. Anakin knew I liked her because he saw us in the bar together so he pursued her himself. She stood no chance. She fell for the sweet talk, the diamonds and the furs. It's hard to resist the champagne lifestyle when you were used to working at the farm all day.

After he had had sex with her, he called me to his bedroom so I would see her in his bed, disheveled and still reeking of him. While he talked to me he moved the sheet that covered her and ran his hand up her thigh. Still watching me, he casually slipped a finger into her and started to finger fuck her.

I could tell she felt horribly embarrassed, but she let him. She thought it was what sophisticated people did. I felt sick to my stomach, but I stood there and let him humiliate me and her. Two days later, he chucked her out without the furs and the diamonds. She went back to North Dakota with her tail between her legs.

I could never take Katya back to Detroit. Never. I'd die first.

"Maybe if I had met you in Moscow, American hunter, things could have been different between us," she whispers.

"There could never be anything between us." My voice cracks like a whip in the silence.

Her eyes widen with shock and a veil comes over her eyes.

I have wounded her. It was never my intention. I am such a fool. My thoughts were ugly with the past and I lashed out without thinking. I reach out a hand to grab her leg, but like a silk scarf she slips out of my grasp and runs to the door. I sit up in bed and I listen to her footsteps running down the corridor. My hands are clenched hard. It is better this way.

It is better this way.

When I hear no more sounds, I go to the window to wait for her. My heart feels as if there is a cold claw squeezing it. She appears underneath the window. I watch her run through the snow. She looks so small and vulnerable. A stranger. I can hardly believe she was the warm, red hot lover in my bed only a few minutes ago.

I want to call out to her, at least to say goodbye, but my throat is locked. God, I want her so bad my chest hurts. Unable to bear even the glass pane to be between me and my last image of her, I open the window. Freezing cold air hits my body. She must have heard the sound because she turns and looks up.

She doesn't wave or smile.

For a while, how long I don't know, we stare at each other. Then she turns away and resumes running towards her ride. I watch till she disappears. I tell myself I won't miss her. I tell myself it's for the best. I could never have given her anything, anyway.

Before I sleep, I picture Katya on the bed, under me, urging me to finish, desperate for me to take away the last bit of girlhood she still had. If this were some movie, I'd leave and come back in a year, and she'd be working in the bar, and I'd stop. She would give me a drink, and we would chat, and then I would leave. In the middle of the night, she would come to my room, and we would make love again. If it were a romantic movie, I would whisk her away from Russia, take her back to America, and make her my bride. If it were a drama, she'd leave after sex, and when I looked for her the next day, she'd be gone. If this were a movie.

But it's not a movie.

KATYA

I know I had to go, but the American could have asked me to stay. Would it have been so bad not to let me feel like a piece of dirt under his shoe? I'm such a fool. Of course, he would want nothing to do with me. I gave away my virginity for nothing. I behaved like a tramp and yet, I cannot feel sorry for it. I will never see him again, but I will never forget tonight.

Never. Not in a million years.

I rush through the snow, meeting no one but a man so drunk he could hardly walk straight. There's a stitch in my side, my breath comes out in great puffs of vapor, and I can feel my heart racing inside my chest. As I round the corner, I see Yuri's truck and the relief that floods through my body is incredible. As it turns out I make it just in time. As I wrap the bear rug around my body and lie low, I hear Yuri come back. He is whistling out of tune and has obviously drunk too much. The ride back is less comfortable than the ride out. For one thing, the hot water bottle is already cold, Yuri's driving is erratic to say the least, but more importantly is the sensation that I am caught in a strange and unreal drama.

I am no longer a virgin.

Tomorrow I will announce the fact to the men who will come to pick me up and they will leave empty-handed. The whole village will be in a state of shock and I know I will probably get hammered by my father. He may even kick me out of the house, but I'm ready for it. I have enough money saved for a bus trip to Moscow. Once I'm there, I will find cheap lodgings and a job. I will be fine. Once the money starts coming into the house, my father and mother will eventually forgive me.

The truck comes to a stop. The engine is cut, then Yuri jumps out and goes into the house, his footsteps quiet in the snow. I dig my way out of the bear skin and as silent as a shadow, I run around to Irina's window. She opens it as soon as I knock on it. I climb into her room and collapse on the floor.

She stands over me, frowning. "Did you do it?"

I nod.

"Why are you so pale? Did he hurt you? Because if he did, I will cut out his tongue and feed it to the crows."

"You will do nothing of the sort. You don't even know who he is. Anyway, he did not hurt me. I'm pale because it is freezing and your brother drives like a maniac."

"Yes, he does, doesn't he? Take your shoes and coat off and get into bed." I obey quickly while she goes to her night table and picks up a blue and green thermos flask. "I made you some hot chocolate," she says, pouring it out into two mugs. Then she joins me on the bed.

I take the steaming drink from her, curling my hands around the warmth. My fingers are like ice cubes.

"Well, how was it then?" she asks, snuggling in beside me. Irina is also a virgin and she has to rely on second hand information.

I bite my lip. "It was amazing."

She nearly sprays me with hot chocolate. "Are you serious?"

I nod.

"Wait a minute? You had sex with some smelly truck driver and it was … amazing?" she asks incredulously.

"It was not a truck driver. It was a foreigner. An American."

She stares at me in astonishment. "What is an American doing around these parts?"

"No idea," I confess. I had been so caught up with everything I hadn't even thought about what he was doing there. He had suddenly appeared, like a character from a Hollywood movie, full of confidence, of his right to be there.

"Come on then. Tell me everything."

So I did. We sat up all night talking. I think we both knew that we would never again, be sharing a bed. No matter what happens in the morning my life is going to change forever.

When dawn breaks over the horizon, Irina hugs me. "I didn't tell you before but my parents put my name down for the program too, but I wasn't chosen. For a while, I was jealous of you then I forgot about it. I'm sorry I thought those things about you. You're brave and strong and I am not. I would never have done what you did. I would have meekly gone even knowing that something bad might happen to me. I'm proud of you, Katya. Really proud of you and no matter what happens, always remember I'm here for you. You can always come here and stay with me."

"Oh, Irina. Thank God, they did not choose you. I couldn't bear it if I thought you were going off never to be seen again. I love you and no matter what happens, you will always be in my heart."

We held each other and cried then.

I left before her parents woke up. I walked in the frosty morning and felt strange as if I wasn't myself. I was walking in someone else's shoes. A girl who had become a woman last night and who was about to walk into the lion's den.

My mother is already up and waiting for me when I walk in through the kitchen door. She looks at me earnestly. In spite of her protestations that I will be completely safe I can tell that she is anxious. Today, I will leave my home and make the trek to a place from which no one has ever returned. It's scary, scarier than she is willing to admit. I can see fear in her face.

"Good. You are back. How are Irina's parents?"

"Fine," I answer.

"Today is your birthday," my mother says, clasping her hands. "They will be coming for you."

"Who will be coming for me?"

My mother frowns then stares at me. "You are still pure, aren't you?"

"And if I'm not? What then, Mama, what then?"

She pales, literally pales. A kind fear I have never before seen fills her eyes. That I might not be pure is beyond her imagination. If she knew what I had done with the American. It was her job to keep me pure and she would have failed.

"You are pure," she cries. "You must be!"

I say nothing.

"Don't you understand? They will beat your father to death for our failure. Then your sister, brother and I will truly be in trouble."

I stare at her. "What do you mean?"

"I mean, we have eaten their money for years. There will be punishment for not delivering."

"What if we pay them back?"

"Pay them back?" she repeated. "Have you gone mad, child? Where will we get that kind of money from?"

"I could go to Moscow. I could work there and send money back. We could pay them bit by bit."

"Katya. What are you saying? Look at you. A country girl who has been sheltered all her life. You know nothing about life in the big city. It is full of violent gangs. Do you know what they do to girls like you? They kidnap them, gang rape and beat them, then traffic them to Europe to work in the worst brothels. I have heard of our girls being forced to sleep with up to forty men a day. And those that do not obey are not killed. They just have their tongues and nipples cut off as a lesson to the other girls."

I take a step back from the horror of the images Mama has drawn.

"But we don't need to be talking about such atrocities … not while you're still pure." Her voice is full of desperation.

I don't answer.

"Tell me you are pure," Mama implores, almost breaking into a sob.

I look into Mama's terrified eyes and I find myself unable to tell what I have done. Not being a virgin is not just the deal-breaker I thought it was, it is actually something that could have tragic and far-reaching consequences. I'm used goods, something the beast who wants me can't abide by. He accepts only the pure. My pretty face won't be enough. I'm sordid and filthy. Although it is possible Mama is exaggerating, I cannot take the chance that Papa will be beaten to death for not doing his job, then Mama, my brother and sister will starve in this little house. I love my family too much.

"Yes, I am still pure," I whisper. I tell myself I will think of some other way to get myself out of this situation. Maybe after the men pick me up I will run away. Then they cannot punish my parents. They did their job properly. The fault will be totally mine. For the moment, I will pretend I'm still a virgin. My parents deserve that.

My mother beams happily at me, all the doubt and fear vanishing like mist in the morning sun. "I never doubted you. Of course not. You are a good girl. A good daughter. Go upstairs and wash while I make you a big birthday breakfast.

Wordlessly, I go into the room I share with my siblings. They are both fast asleep. I take off my coat, crawl under the covers, and close my eyes. What a mess. I wonder if I can hide a knife in my bag. It won't do much, but a knife is a good thing to have. I think I can use it if I have to.

KATYA

My breakfast is two fried eggs, the yolks unbroken, topped with sliced sausages, cheese; and blinis with wild honey. It's my mother's acknowledgment of my birthday. With the plate of food comes a card, something purchased from a store. This is something I should keep because it will be my last birthday in my little town. I know that.

My parents know that too and they're trying their best to make something of this birthday. My father gives me a kiss on the head, and that's the first one in a year. It's his way of showing that he's proud of me. My mother prompted him, but I don't care. It's his last kiss. There are a lot of 'lasts' today.

In fact, if I believe Mrs. Komarov, this will be the last I will see or hear of these people again, and that isn't even taking into consideration the added complication of my lack of a hymen. I catch my mother staring at me and I can see worry lines on her face. She isn't sure anymore that I'm still the little virgin girl she raised. I smile back confidently because I don't want her to feel bad. I don't want her to worry. I won't spoil her day. I won't spoil her dream of living the next five years in relative luxury.

But there will be no more money coming unless I find a way to get a job and send it. I am not afraid of the city. Thousands of girls leave their villages and end up in the cities. They all don't end up in the hands of traffickers. Somehow, I will survive. I'm old enough to do anything I want.

For a moment, I remember the night before, the sex.

The American came along at just the right moment, right for me. I gave myself freely and I suspect that it will be the last time that happens. From now on, I'll never give myself like that again. I'll never give another man the chance to make me feel so cheap and used. Last night, I had wished the American would have ordered me to stay with him. Taken me by the hand and walked me to his car, or the train station or wherever. I wish we were now on our way to the embassy. It wouldn't matter where. I wish it had happened that way. The American seemed to know me better than I know myself.

I can't believe I'm actually missing him. Stupid.

Because he clearly doesn't want me. That hurts most of all. When I really examine it, he treated me badly. He took what he wanted and then turned me out. While I'm angry, I can't be too upset. I was the one who chose to go to his room. I was the one who saw my actions as a way to avoid my fate. It was me, not him, but he could have acted better.

He could have been kinder.

After breakfast, I go back to my room and get ready for the trip. Both my brother and sister sit on my bed and watch me packing. They're somber and quiet. I try to lighten the mood, but I don't feel too happy myself. My wardrobe is meagre, but I don't take much. I leave my best dress for my sister. She starts sobbing when I give it to her. I tell her I will buy better ones in America.

She brightens up at that. "Will you buy a dress for me too?"

"Of course," I say with a big smile.

"What about me? Tatyana already has more clothes than me," my brother complains.

"Tatyana is always going to have more clothes than you. You better get used to it," I tell him. "But if Mama tells me you were a good boy, I'll send an American toy for you."

His eyes light up. "What kind of toy?"

"Oh, I don't know. I'll have to see what boys your age play with in America."

He clasps his hands together with joy.

It occurs to me then that I should only run away once I am in America. The thought electrifies me. Maybe I could make this work.

At that moment, Mama calls my siblings to help her bring in the firewood so they run off.

I place the last item I own into my bag and look at my face in the mirror. I haven't dressed in my best clothes, but something that will keep me warm and is suitable for travelling. I know I don't need to look good for whoever comes for me. I doubt they will care one way or the other. I'm just some woman to be picked up, hauled away and delivered some-place else.

I pull out all my money from its hiding place underneath the floorboard and carefully hide it in a secret pocket inside my clothes. If I manage to escape, I will need it. Then I take a last look around my small room. The crucifix over my bed reminds me I committed a sin last night, but I don't feel particularly guilty. I had a good reason for my sinful behavior. There is a short stack of books in the corner. I've read them all several times; they brought comfort on the long, winter nights.

When I was younger and even more stupid than I am now, I thought I could have a storybook life. Prince Charming would come and sweep me away. I'd live in a big house with maids and servants ... the best of everything. They're just stories, just fantasies.

This is reality.

My leaving is reality.

I walk over to the bureau I share with my brother and sister to look at the picture of St. Therese, the patron saint of Russia. My mother hung it there to remind us to be good children. I'm afraid I haven't lived up to St. Therese's standards, but St. Therese never had to march off to slavery with a smile on her face. I make the sign of the cross and close the doors. I've wasted enough time in my room.

I should go downstairs and make my final goodbyes.

On the table, there is a small Western style birthday cake, the type that is only sold in a nearby town. My heart aches. My parents must have saved for weeks in order to afford the extravagance.

My sister is jumping up and down with excitement and my

brother is licking his lips. Smiling, my mother lights the single candle. My father leads in the singing of "Happy Birthday" but my sister's voice is the loudest.

I feel tears sting the backs of my eyes. It's not only happy birthday but goodbye. We all know that. When the song ends, I go to blow out the candle, but my sister screams for me to make a wish first. And though I know wishes are for fools. They never come true. I close my eyes and make a wish. A crazy stupid wish. I wish for the American. I open my eyes and blow out the candle. I might as well have asked for Prince Charming to rush into the house and carry me off to the castle.

There is no gift. The cake is my gift.

My mother cuts me a generous piece. It's good cake and it's the last cake they will ever give me. From now on, they won't be there for me. I'll have to take care of myself. I look at my brother and sister greedily scoffing their slices and the benevolence in my father's eyes. I feel sadness well up inside me. When I was younger, I thought leaving the village would make me giddy with joy. Who wouldn't want to escape this? Now that I'm about to leave, I desperately want to hold onto this.

I blink hard and my mother looks at me with tears in her own eyes. My father bites his lip.

At that moment, I realize they both know what is going to happen to me, but are too poor and helpless to change it. For one wild second, I stare at them and I wish one of them would simply refuse to honor the arrangement. I wish they would defend their daughter with their very lives. But both my unhappy parents let their eyes slide away. Suddenly, I feel so hurt I want to leave immediately, before the scene becomes something I will regret. As if on cue, there's a loud knock on the door.

Everybody freezes.

My captors are here.

Then my father walks towards the door, his shoulders are stooped and he looks old beyond his years.

The first man to enter is tall, gaunt and old. He has a typical Russian face, long and morose. It usually means they're sober. It's only when they drink that they come to life. Drunk, they are almost jovial. The man moves forward because he's followed by a second man.

My blood runs cold. What the …?

The American!

KATYA

I stare at him in shock. Am I asleep and dreaming? What is he doing here? He's the last person I expected. The men who came for the girls were always Russian. Then our eyes meet and I know it isn't a dream. It is a nightmare.

He's surprised too. I can see that in his eyes. And there's something else in his eyes too. Confusion. I can guess why. He's here to pick up a virgin and he knows I'm no longer that. My heart jumps into my throat. If he says something, then this house of cards will collapse, and my parents will be punished. I can't allow that to happen. I can't let on that we have met. That would be disastrous.

I move past the tall man as he talks to my parents in Russian. "I'm Katya," I say to the American in English.

He stares at me, not understanding. "I'm Hunter."

"And your friend, does he speak English?"

"A little."

I glance at the other man. He's not paying any attention to us. "We have never met," I whisper. "OK?"

He nods and I think he understands the game. We have to fool my parents and the older man. We have to make them think that this is our first meeting.

My mother tells me that she and father are going outside to talk to the older man. They will be back in a minute. No doubt, they are going to talk about money.

As soon as they disappear, he turns on me. "What the hell is going on?" he demands.

"That was what I was going to ask you?"

"Last night, you knew I was here for you, didn't you?"

"I had no idea," I say truthfully. "If I had known, I would have left with one of the other men." That's a lie and I think it hurts him a little. I suppose he considers himself well above the likes of the local. He is, but I don't care to tell him that.

He shakes his head in wonder. "So you're what this is all about?"

"What do you mean?"

"I was told I was going to pick up a package, not a person."

I can't believe him. How could he come all this way and not know he was gathering up a slave? "It has been happening for twenty years," I tell him. "Once a year, a man named Anakin takes a girl from one of the five villages that have agreed to take part in the program. It is on a rotation basis. The girl is never heard from again. The parents get a stipend, but that is all."

His eyes narrow and I get the feeling that he is dangerous. Far more than what I knew. "You're kidding. What, you're the twentieth?"

I nod. "The fourth virgin from the village and the twentieth in the program."

He steps back. "You're supposed to be a virgin?"

"Shhhh," I hiss. "You know what I was yesterday, and you know what I am today. If your friend finds out, things will go badly."

He stares at me, his eyes hard and a frown on his forehead, and I can see him trying to process this information. He's not been involved before, so I like to think maybe if he'd known, he wouldn't be here now. He would refuse to pick up a slave. Maybe he will help me escape.

"I have agreed to go," I tell him. "I'm not going to tell anyone about last night. I trust you won't mention it either. Please."

"What the fuck, Katya?"

"Think about it," I say. "I can deny it happened and that might work. Worse for you, I can say you forced me. What would Anakin think about that? What if he knew it was you who ruined me?"

"Don't threaten me," he says. "That won't work."

"Then, work with me," I say. "For me and my parents. Work with me. I won't tell anyone it was you."

He doesn't answer, but at that moment, my parents and the older man return. Apparently, the deal has been struck; the slave has been paid for. With my own smile, I go to my parents and hug them. My mother cries and whispers to me to be a good girl. My father holds me a moment longer than usual and I can hear his heart beating. I think I will miss him more than I thought I would.

When I turn from my parents, I see that the American has grabbed my bag. The older man assures my parents that they will hear from me soon. I could call him a liar, but that would do little good. The parents of the other girls have heard nothing. I don't really believe that my fate will be so different.

Still, I'm thankful the American has chosen to play along with me. If he were to tell the truth … well, he hasn't. That's a good thing. That means I have a chance. Maybe I can convince him to help me escape. I grab my purse and I don't look back. There are tears in my eyes and I would rather not have my parents see that. I don't know why. My sister rushes to me and hugs me from behind. I close my eyes and clench my jaw to stop from crying. A few seconds later, my brother joins her.

I take a deep breath and turn around. I kneel. "Everything will be fine. Be good for Mama and Papa."

My brother starts sobbing. "I don't want any American toys. Just don't go."

I cannot stop the tears that fill my eyes and pour down my face.

My mother comes up to us. "Let your sister go—now." Her voice breaks.

I stand and look into her eyes. I lean forward and hug her, while my lips are close to her ear, I say, "Whatever you do, don't ever enroll Tatyana in the program." Then I straighten.

She nods as tears run down her face.

Wordlessly, I turn around and walk away. I feel numb inside.

The two men walk on either side of me.

The American opens the car door of a rust colored car for me and I slip inside. Our bodies brush. How strange that despite my terrible situation there's still lust inside me for him. I remember how he looks naked. Even though his skin is full of rough tattoos and scars, they cannot mar the splendor of his hard body. Even now if I think of how strong or how powerful he is, I know I will get a little rush. We will be travelling together, but with the other man around, we will not be together at all.

The men get inside and the car starts to pull away. I turn to look at my family gathered outside. I wave and pray it isn't the last time I will see them. The car drives away, but my sister starts running after us. She runs until she slips on a patch of ice and falls. I don't say or do anything. I watch her get up and try to chase us, but her figure becomes smaller and smaller until I see her no more.

In the sky the sun shines a buttery yellow. It shouldn't.

HUNTER

I'm so fucking bewildered I can't even think straight. Disjointed thoughts fly into my head until my mind is a whirling black tornado of confusion and shock. The dream girl from last night is the package! What the fuck? How the hell? No way. Just no.

She's Anakin's girl. I remember his fat, white fingers moving in and out of Mary Jane's little pussy. No! Heck no!

Every cell, every atom in my body rejects the vile idea. She's mine. Not his. I stare at the snowy road, unseeing, my hands clenched tight while my mind replays what Katya told me. Anakin has been getting virgins for the last twenty years. How could that be? How come I never saw any of them?

I lived in his cellar for ten years, but I was always allowed out for an hour. When he was away on business his old servant would take pity on me and let me roam the house on my own. I never saw any signs of anyone else living in the house. And once I was fifteen and he knew for sure he had broken me and turned me into his obedient dog, I was allowed to live in his annex, where I still live now. What the fuck has he done to all these girls? What is he going to do with Katya?

My mobile rings, making me jump. I pull it out of my pocket. It is Anakin. My blood turns to ice.

"Have you picked up my package?" he demands.

"Yes," the word is torn painfully out of my throat.

"Good."

In that one word I hear something I have never heard before. Relish and hidden need. It creeps me out. Suddenly, he is Gollum in the blue light of the cave, his scratchy voice saying, "*We wants it. We needs it. Must have the Precious. Sneaky little hobbitses. They stole it from us. Wicked. Tricksy, False.*"

My brain feels like it is on fire. I can't hand over Precious to Gollum, but then his voice changes and he becomes the Anakin I know. My master. "I paid a lot of money for her, so I hope I can count on you to do this job well."

I don't know how it happens, but it is as if there is a switch inside my head that Anakin can turn on and off. One that only he can access. The need to please him is stronger than any other instinct I have. Even the need for self-preservation or to protect an innocent human being from a depraved predator. I hear myself saying robotically, "Yes, you can count on me."

"Good. Good. When you are back, I'll take you out to dinner. It'll be like old times."

"Yes," I reply quietly.

"Call me when you get to Moscow."

"All right."

The line goes dead. My chest feels tight, but I don't have a whirling tornado in my head anymore. My role is very simple. I came here to pick up a package. All I have to do is escort it back to Detroit. It is a simple job. My mind throws up the scent of the girl as she lay, her legs open, her naked pussy inches from my nose. I push the thought away and simply remind myself that she belongs to Anakin.

I'm just the guy who will deliver her.

My face feels strangely hot, so I wind down the window. A gust of cold wind bites right through the sleeve of my leather jacket. Icy snowflakes hit my skin. I turn my feverish face towards the sun shining like a pale ball in the clear sky, but Sherpa has already warned us that a storm is coming. If I look over my shoulder, the clouds coming toward us are dark, very dark.

The train station is around the corner and I think I'll be happier when we are safe on the train, flying across the countryside while watching the snow through a window. I inhale deeply and fill my lungs with the clean fresh air and slowly, slowly, my mind clears. She's off limits, as if she's diseased. I have to remember that. She's not mine. She was never mine. This isn't a movie. In real life, precious belongs to the Gollums of this world. What happened last night was just a mistake. A terrible mistake. She's as much a victim as I am.

I'll find a way to talk to her when the Sherpa goes out for a smoke. We'll talk about what the hell this whole thing is all about. What she plans to do. Anakin is expecting a virgin.

The train station is deserted. That includes the platform.

There aren't any passengers milling about. This feels very bad. The Sherpa says something to Katya, but it is too fast for me to understand, and heads for the ticket office.

She turns to me. "He's going to check out what's going on."

I frown. I don't have a good feeling.

"This is a small town, and a small station. Sometimes, it goes on through, or it is late. It is not unusual."

"If that's the case, when is the next train?"

"Tomorrow … maybe."

"That's a hell of a way to run a railroad."

She shrugs. "It saves money. At least, that's what they say."

"Look," I say. "About last night—"

"Nothing happened last night. Nothing. If you cannot keep your tongue still, I will tell the Sherpa to leave you behind. He will do it because I am what he came for."

"I hate to break this to you, missy, but he's just the local talent. You're flying back to Detroit with me. So, there's no way, the Sherpa—"

"Sherpa?"

"That's what I call him because he didn't introduce himself and he's my guide here, but once we get to Moscow, he'll disappear."

"Please. Don't say anything now. We can talk."

"Okay, we will pretend last night didn't happen, but when we get some time alone, and we will, you're going to tell me what this business is all about. Then we will work out what we are going to do about this situation. Anakin isn't someone you want to play with. Got that?"

"I understand that," she says solemnly. In the light from the windows her long curly hair glints as if she is a sixteenth century heroine.

My stomach contracts painfully. I nod and turn away from her.

"Now, quiet, Boris … the Sherpa is coming back," she whispers.

I turn around to look at her in surprise and she smiles to show me she appreciates my little joke. It's a small thing in a very bad situation, but I smile back. In the pale light, we smile at each other like fools.

The Sherpa approaches us. He looks annoyed. "There will be no train today."

"Should we book into a hotel?" I ask.

The Sherpa shakes his head violently. "No. That's not part of the plan. Wait here," he orders shortly before striding off.

I turn back to Katya. "Tell me about this virgin deal."

"Every five years, the town sends a virgin to Anakin. It's always on her eighteenth birthday, so she is legally an adult. In the five years before that, he sends the parents money. Not a lot of money, but even a small amount is large here. And afterwards, Anakin sends more money and a lifelong stipend. The family lives better than ever."

"What does he do with the girls?"

She scowls. "No one knows, but they're never heard from again. Most of the girls are very good girls, respectable girls, they wouldn't abandon their families so easily, so there cannot be a reasonable excuse why they do not write home even a single sentence to say they're fine."

I have to agree with her. Not hearing from them is a problem. Because I've been with Anakin for as long as I can remember, and I've never heard anything about a virgin imported from Russia. None of his men talk about it either. If it was on the grapevine, I would have heard. Something doesn't smell right to me, but I know Anakin is capable of almost anything. He's done some nasty things to people who don't make their payments. Perverted things. Things that would turn an ordinary man's stomach.

"What if he sells me to some rich Arab who turns me into his slave?"

I know instantly that isn't the fate awaiting her. Anakin isn't selling her to anyone. Until I can figure this out I don't want to panic her. "I don't think Anakin even knows a rich Arab." I keep my voice mild.

"Everyone knows a rich Arab. They like to buy whatever they want."

I doubt she has ever seen an Arab, let alone a rich one. I haven't. "I tell you what. When we get back to the states, I'll make sure your parents know you made it. I promise that. They won't have to guess where you are or what happened to you."

"Don't make promises you cannot keep," she shoots back.

"I keep my promises."

"Everyone says that, until they cannot keep them. This is Russia, promises are cheap."

Her attitude annoys me at a primitive level. I've lived my whole life believing promises are sacred. You make one, you keep it. It's that simple. I'm good on my word, no matter what. I told Anakin I would bring her back for him and I will, but then I stare into her beautiful eyes and it's hard to even think straight.

"The Sherpa is no fool," she continues. "So don't look at me like that or he'll notice."

That's good, Katya. Stay hostile. We need to be enemies or I could never resist you. "If I don't chat you up, the Sherpa will think I'm gay," I respond dryly.

She laughs without humor. "Believe me, the Sherpa knows exactly what you like."

I have to agree with her. The Sherpa might like me—in a very Russian way—but he's loyal only to Anakin. Not that I'd ever test a man's loyalty. That's a recipe for disaster. The men who have tested my loyalty have all gone on to meet their maker.

In the periphery of my vision I see the Sherpa waving to us from a distance.

"The Sherpa beckons," I tell her, cutting our chat off.

She doesn't answer, just starts off by herself. I grab the bag and follow. I watch her ass as she moves off, and I remember how it felt in my hands. I remember how smooth her skin is, how pure. I remember how she crawls and licks my erection. I remember, and the lust burns fresh inside me. Fuck! She's not mine. I'm not allowed to look at her with desire oozing out my skin. Gone, gone, gone ... I tell the persistent thoughts to be gone.

Outside, the Sherpa points to an aged Ford Explorer. "We go to Moscow."

I look over at the vehicle. It's faded, dented, covered with dirt, and two of the tires are almost bald. It looks as if it's on its last legs. There's a long crack along the rear window, and when I try the latch, it doesn't work. I can't get it open. The Sherpa points to a rear door, and I jerk it open. The interior is as dingy and ripped as the exterior. I throw in Katya's bag as the Sherpa tells Katya to get in the front as he climbs behind the wheel.

Inside, the Sherpa starts an engine that sounds as if the muffler fell off many years ago. I hope the exhaust doesn't leak into the cabin.

"Ford," the Sherpa says. "Much better than Russian cars."

This Explorer might have been stellar when it was first put together, but at this point, it's a rattle-trap, something that should be politely rusting away in some junk yard. I'm guessing Russians harvest parts. In fact, I'm guessing that they harvest every bit they can put to use. With any luck, most of the working parts in this vehicle have been replaced recently. Otherwise, we're as close to Moscow as we'll ever be.

"How long till we get to Moscow?"

"Two days," he replies.

"How? It's three days by train."

"The car is faster," he says. "Four-wheel driver."

"Yeah," I mutter. "Four-wheel driver."

The day grows darker as we leave Sutgot. The snow is visible through the dirty windows. Up front, the Sherpa and the girl seem totally oblivious to the snow. I have a knot in my stomach, a gut feeling that we should have stayed in a hotel, but I tell myself to stop worrying. If the Russians aren't worried, why should I be? I grab the bag and toss it into the very back where there's a bald spare tire. I lie down across the seat and pull my jacket tight. Closing my eyes, I try to think, but I can't concentrate because the vehicle is bouncing, slipping and sliding like crazy.

Opening my eyes, I look for a seat belt. There isn't one. Up front, they're not using seat belts either.

"We outrun snow," I hear the Sherpa say.

"Yeah," I say back. "Outrun snow."

KATYA

I find it difficult to believe an experienced, old hand like the Sherpa ... I have adopted the American's title ... rented this death trap. It looks like it will fall apart if it hits anything heavier than a snowflake.

I have no expectations of making it to Moscow. It is simply a matter of where it will break down. If we are close to a town, he might get a chance to rent another vehicle.

Despite what the Sherpa says, we will not outrun the snow. It will cover us before we get anywhere near Moscow. If my father was here he would say the Sherpa is an idiot for being out in this foul weather, but it might be my best hope of escaping. If I see even the smallest chance of making a run for it, I will take it.

The snow falls thicker with every passing minute. It will be dark soon, and all the car has are these small, weak lights. I hope we are close to a town. I don't like our chances in this car. Luckily, the road is straight. That much is good, but it's not a good road. The vehicle rattles with every bounce. Even the radio doesn't work.

I think the Sherpa is driving by feel, and even as I watch, the car starts to spin and he immediately turns the steering wheel in the opposite direction. At least he doesn't have a death wish. He slows right down and squinting into the driving snow, he pulls out a cigarette and lights it. The car fills with smoke.

I hit the button for the window, but it doesn't work. It seems very little works in this vehicle. He notices and lowers his window a little, and the smoke goes his way. I'm grateful, but I won't tell him. I know there's no use trying to butter him up. Such things don't work with old Russian men. They will take what you give and then do as they please anyway.

The Sherpa glances back at the American. He's lying down and his eyes are closed. The Sherpa shakes his head and tells me that he thinks the American is big but worthless. I ask him why he thinks this, and he says all Americans are weak and lazy. They have too much, so they work too little. It's nature. Any animal that eats without working grows fat and lazy. It doesn't matter if it's a rat or a human. Too much leads to weakness. The Americans have too much.

He says the American brought a prostitute back to his hotel room the night before. The noise that bitch made kept him up for hours. He throws his cigarette butt and spits out of the window before winding the glass up again.

I could tell the Sherpa that the American in the backseat is not flabby or soft. He's rock hard and powerful. Perhaps, he's not one of the pampered people the Sherpa knows. But if I tell the Sherpa that, he'll want to know how I know so much about the American. Then I will have to tell him that the bitch who kept him from his sleep with all her cries and screams was me.

I turn away from him and stare at the snow. We seem to be the only ones foolhardy enough to be on the road, but in a way, the lack of traffic is a good thing. The Sherpa won't be crashing into another vehicle.

He lights a second cigarette, and I can tell he's getting a bit nervous. The snow and dark are getting to him. To be honest, it's all getting to me too. But there is no place to stop out here in the hinterland. I don't know much about my country, but I know there is little development around here. This may be the least populated place in all of Russia—except for Siberia. No one lives in Siberia except the criminals placed there.

With the cigarette comes more talk. It's almost as if the Sherpa is drinking, and after every vodka he has to make some pronouncement. This one is about the corrupt officials in Moscow. He hates them. They steal money from everyone, especially him. They're blood suckers, and they drain the life from everything they touch.

If he had his way, they would be marched out of their offices and summarily shot. He would bulldoze a big pit and dump the bodies without funerals or ceremonies. Then, he would cover up the bodies and plant flowers. At least their rotting bodies would provide food for something pretty. As he rambles on while peering at the windscreen and puffing out smoke like a dragon, I realize that the Sherpa is more than a little bit crazy. On a night like this, being driven by a mad man isn't a good thing. When we crash, I must make sure to go with the American.

Bruno will surely lead me into a blizzard and abandon me.

It happens when the Sherpa tries to toss his dying cigarette out the window. He doesn't lower the glass far enough, and the butt bounces off the window and into his lap. He should have his testicles burnt off for being so klutzy, as he flaps around between his legs for the still glowing butt. As he does that, he takes his concentration off the road, his hand turns the wheel, and in seconds, we're clipping off a reflector on our way into a field of white. There isn't time to correct the steering. I grab the door handle and hope we don't bang into a tree.

Bouncing through the ditch enlightens the Sherpa as to our predicament. He forgets about his roasting balls and jerks the wheel back toward the road, but he's too late. We're deep in the snow, and the spinning wheels do nothing but dig a deeper hole. We don't move an inch and while the side of my head hurts from where it hit the window, I'm all right. I rub my head as the Sherpa puts the vehicle in reverse and tries to back out.

Nothing.

"What the fuck was that?" the American asks from the back.

The Sherpa curses in Russian, which is good. If the American understood what the Sherpa was saying, there might be a fight.

"We're off the road," I tell the American.

"I can see that. How did we get here?"

"It happened when he tried to toss his cigarette out of the window and missed."

The Sherpa curses even more colorfully and spins the wheels again. It rocks the vehicle a little, but it's certain that we're not going anywhere.

"Tell him I'm getting out to push," the American says. "Maybe we can get back to the road."

I could have told the American not to bother. We're too far off the road, and the snow is falling too fast, but both men seem to think they know better. Besides, I haven't forgiven the American for the way he brushed me off last night. Let him find himself on the side of stupid for a change.

As he climbs out, I tell the Sherpa what's happening.

He grunts and calls the American a pea green jester. In Russia, this is a derogatory expression. It is supposed to recall the image of a jester from Medieval Europe wearing a pair of donkey ears and carrying a rattle made of a bull's bladder filled with dried peas. Basically, he was calling the American a moron or an idiot.

I wait, trying to stay warm and sane. As the Sherpa rocks the vehicle, I can feel the American push, but it does no good. Once he manages to get the vehicle out of its ruts, it only moves a few feet before bogging down again.

The Sherpa tells me to drive as he climbs out to join the American. I tell him I don't drive, and he tells me with great irritation it's not driving, it's holding the damn steering wheel and pushing on the gas while they push. Biting back a sarcastic reply, I do as I'm told, and moments later, he's at the back with the American. I press on the gas, and they push. The vehicle moves a few more feet before the wheels spin and the car comes to a stop. From there, it will do nothing. A few minutes later, they both return to their seats.

The Sherpa and the American shiver and blow on their hands. This isn't a night to be out and they both know it. They're also aware the vehicle isn't going anywhere for a while.

"How long before someone comes along?" the American asks.

The Sherpa says on a night like this, it might be hours.

The American doesn't like the answer. He pulls out his phone.

I let him look for service without saying a word. I know there is none. We're far from any tower that might provide a connection.

"What a fucking country," he says as he puts his phone into his pocket.

The Sherpa tells us that we cannot stay in the vehicle. Even if we conserve the fuel, we will eventually freeze. We must find a better shelter.

The American disagrees. In America, people stay with their cars because it's stupid to roam out in the thick of a storm. We could be going in circles. The Sherpa doesn't care. He tells us that he noticed a lane as we left the road. While the lane is unused, it must lead to some kind of shelter. And that shelter cannot be far. It will be better there than here since the snow will soon cover the tracks we made. No one will notice till the storm is long gone.

The American doesn't like the message, but he has little choice. This is Russia, and the Sherpa is in command. The American agrees to go a little further, but not too far. If we don't find something in fifteen minutes, we should come back while we can still see our footprints.

Fifteen minutes in this snow will take us perhaps a kilometer, and I agree that if the shelter isn't within a kilometer, we should return. Wandering around in the dark and snow will certainly kill us. The Sherpa doesn't agree, but he doesn't have to. The American seems to have taken over, even though this is the Sherpa's territory.

The wind is strong, but it isn't yet at blizzard speed. We can walk and going single file along our own tracks is fine. The Sherpa finds the lane, and turns into the unmarred snow. I bow my head into the blowing, thick snow and slog after the Sherpa. As he plows ahead, I follow, stretching my legs to land my feet in his tracks. That makes it easier. I know the American is behind me even though I can't see him.

For a moment, I wonder if dying in a blizzard will be my fate, but I know the American is keeping track. I'm pretty sure the snow is not falling so thickly that it will cover our tracks in fifteen minutes.

The American shouts that we have reached our time limit. The Sherpa stops and looks back. The American comes around and stands by the Sherpa who points up ahead. I follow the direction he is pointing to. There in the snow is the dark outline of a house, or, barn or some kind of wooden structure.

We all see it. But it's the American who takes the lead now. I move around the Sherpa who takes up the rear gratefully. Leading through the snow is a job for a dog, not a man. I find it slightly easier to step into the American's prints. It is as if he is deliberately keeping his stride small to make it less demanding for me. In minutes, we reach what was once a house, is still a kind of house. As I step onto the porch, the American tries the door. It's locked.

He pounds at it, but there are no lights, and I'm certain no one is inside. This is just the remnant of some dream, the last dregs of a wish.

The Sherpa joins the American and between the two of them, they manage to force the door open. I hurry past them into the house, thankful for the shelter. The Sherpa closes the door as the American turns on his phone and shines its light around the room.

What we see is encouraging.

The room isn't completely bare. There's a table with chairs and beyond that a kitchen with cabinets and a sink with a pump. On one side is a fireplace, and beside it, a few old logs. There are two other closed doors that must be a bedroom and perhaps a bathroom. I have no hope of running water, but we have lots of snow that we can melt. If we are lucky, the pump will work. If we are unlucky, we will do our business outside in the snow. I do not relish that probability, but it is a small matter compared to freezing to death in a ditch.

"Check out those rooms," the American tells me.

As I head for the door, I hear him talk to the Sherpa. "Get your lighter out. We need to start a fire."

The first room is the bedroom. While the bed and other furniture are gone, there is an old mattress on the floor. It's not much, but it might be something we can use. I check the small closet. It's bare. I had hoped that perhaps a blanket or two might be left behind. We aren't that lucky.

The second room is the bathroom, and while there is a sink, bath and toilet, there is no water. If the pump in the kitchen doesn't work, the bathroom is useless. In the half light from the other room, I look at myself in the cloudy mirror. I don't look so good tonight. I laugh. The sound comes out wild and a little scary. "Get a hold of yourself, Katya," I tell my reflection sternly before turning away.

Back in the main room, the Sherpa and the American have managed to light a small fire from some paper scraps. The Sherpa takes an old log and slams it on the floor, trying to split it. It is dry and breaks apart easily, then he adds the small pieces to the fire.

I know that in five minutes we'll have enough light and heat to survive—at least for the time being. And it's only the time being I'm worried about. I move to the fire and crouch in front of it. It will take a lot of fire to heat this house, and we don't have enough logs, but I am guessing there will be some outside.

The American goes to the pump and jacks the handle up and down several times. No water comes out, but he doesn't seem disgusted. The Sherpa tells him the pump needs to be primed. The American isn't quite sure what priming is, and I realize he's never experienced a pump before. He's a city man. He's never dealt with life in the country. That might be a very bad thing at this point.

Luckily, the Sherpa knows what to do. He looks for something that will hold water, and he finds nothing but small glasses and cracked cups. We can melt snow, but he's not going to worry about that. Instead, he climbs into the sink and pees down the pump, priming it with piss.

I turn away. That's the last thing I want to see.

But it works.

After he pees, he works the pump, and rusty water comes out. He keeps pumping until the water turns clear, and he turns to us with a smile on his face. He's managed to give us the thing we need most—water in the toilet.

The American smiles.

We're making progress.

"There's a mattress in the bedroom," I tell the American.

The American doesn't need to be told twice. He goes into the bedroom and drags out the mattress which he sets before the thriving fire.

I sit on it because it's softer and will be warmer than the floor.

The Sherpa tells us he's going to walk around the house and see if there's wood or something else useful.

After he's gone, I turn to the American, and I speak softly. I don't think the Sherpa can hear, but I want to be careful, "I don't think this is good."

HUNTER

She looks at me with real concern on her face, and I know what she's thinking. This is crap. Yes, we have water and shelter and a fire, but there's no food, and no one is looking for us. Even if someone finds the vehicle, they probably won't find us. We're too far away, and our tracks are probably snowed over already. But there's nothing to be done at the moment, we can't go back to the vehicle and we can't contact anyone. We're stuck, at least till the snow stops.

"It isn't good," I tell her. "It's terrible, but we can't do anything about it. We're lucky to have this much."

"If we run out of wood, we'll freeze to death."

"We have a table and chairs that will burn and if need be, we'll rip up the cabinets. I think we have enough for a day or two. That should be enough. We won't starve in a day or two."

"What will your boss say when you miss your flight?"

I shrug. "Anakin will be pissed, but that doesn't matter. We have a good excuse."

"And when he discovers I'm no longer a virgin?"

It is the one thing I cannot stop thinking about. Anakin will be royally pissed, enough to hurt not just me but the girl too. He won't kill me, I'm too useful to him, but it may be worth a few broken bones and new scars. "He'll accept it," I lie.

"Unless he thinks you did it."

She thinks she has cut to the heart of the matter. She thinks Anakin is a reasonable man. Once it is discovered she isn't a virgin, well, then, I'll be the culprit whether or not it is my fault. I'm the whipping post, the little kid with his hand in the cookie jar. "Well," I say with a shrug, "If you're up to it, you can tell him how I picked you up while you are at it."

She considers that a moment. "Then, my parents will suffer. They won't get the stipend. I will have to say you forced me."

"You can try saying that if you want, but he won't believe it," I say softly. Anakin knows I'd rather die than betray him. "I'm sorry, Katya. No matter how you spin it this story will not have a happy ending."

She stares at me in astonishment. "So you're just going to hand me over to a complete monster."

Something primitive inside me growls at the thought, but I nod slowly.

"I was wrong about you. I thought you were a gentleman. I thought you were different than all those men in that bar. But you're not different, are you? You're just a selfish pig. You care only about your own skin. What kind of man—"

She stops abruptly when the front door is suddenly kicked open and the Sherpa comes through the door with an armload of snowy firewood. He staggers to the fireplace and dumps them on the ground.

I close the door against the snow and cold. He mutters something in Russian that I don't catch, but Katya tells me that there's more wood by the side of the house. It looks like I won't have to rip apart the cabinets.

The Sherpa leans against the mantel for a moment before he pulls out a cigarette. He lights it and inhales then starts across the room. That's when the cigarette drops from his hand. For a second he does nothing, just turns to me with a bewildered expression almost child-like expression on his old face.

"What is it?" I ask.

He opens his mouth and a string of colorful curses unfurl from his mouth. Suddenly, his hand rises up to clutch his chest and a strangled cry of pain emits from his swearing mouth. Before I can do a thing, he keels over, his body falling on the hard floor with a dull thud.

I recognize a heart attack when I see one, and I move as fast as I can. I roll the Sherpa onto his back. He looks up at the ceiling in wonder as if he could see the stars in the sky while the muscles of his throat moves valiantly as if trying to express his vision.

I open his coat and his shirt then start compressions. I'm not sure I'm doing them correctly. This is a new one for me. I have no experience reviving a man, only taking his life. I stop pumping for a second and listen for a heartbeat, but I don't hear anything.

When I look up, the girl gapes at me. I don't think she's ever seen anyone die. We all do it, but most of us are a little more polite about it than the Sherpa. I learned a lot of new curses in the last minutes of his life.

"Get some water," I tell her.

She doesn't move. She stands there frozen.

"Water!" I bark.

She moves jerkily away, and I keep working. I don't think we really need water, but it gives her something to do besides gape at me. I was once told that in an emergency, everyone should be given some sort of job to do to keep that person from freaking out. One disaster is enough. I don't watch her. I keep pressing on the Sherpa's chest.

"Come on," I tell him. "Come on, you're not ready to die yet. No one is. Take a breath. Kickstart that pump. Get the blood flowing."

My talk is more for me than for the Sherpa. His eyes are open, but there is a blankness to them that gives me the impression he has already gone to join his ancestors, but there is always a possibility that he could come back with a cough. I've seen that happen in movies.

Katya returns with a glass of water. Her face is as white as a sheet. She kneels beside me. "What do you want me to do?"

"Put down the water," I tell her. "And feel his neck for a pulse."

She feels for a pulse. If his heart is working, she'll feel something. She shakes her head, her lips are trembling.

"Put another log on the fire," I say, giving her another job to do.

Then, I go back to pumping. *Come on old man. I could really do with your guidance in the back of nowhere.* I hear the log land on the fire.

"You can't conk out," I tell the Sherpa. "Who is gonna drive that pile of bolts you call a damn car? It can't be me. They catch me driving without a license and they'll send me to a gulag."

"There are no more gulags." Katya stands and frowns. "At least, I don't think there are any."

I'm not going to argue. I save my breath for the pumping. She comes back and kneels next to me.

"Feel for a pulse again."

As she feels, I strip off my jacket. The pumping is making me sweaty, and sweat isn't a good thing in this environment.

She shakes her head again.

"I'm going to give him two more minutes," I tell her. "Then, we'll just see what happens."

She nods and I go back to work. We don't speak as I drive down on his unresponsive chest. The Sherpa doesn't start to breathe. His eyes remain fixed on the ceiling. I'm certain he's dead, but if you don't want someone to give up on you, you don't give up on them. I keep going for the full two minutes. At the end of the two minutes, I listen for a beat.

Nothing.

I lean back and look at her. "He's dead," I say just to make it final.

She knows the truth, which is plain. "I know." She sounds very calm. It could be shock or a Russian thing. I'll find out soon enough.

I move away from the Sherpa and walk to a chair. I don't need to sit by the fire. I'm already too hot. Katya doesn't join me. She slumps down on the mattress by the fire. We are both lost in our own thoughts for a while. We've lost our guide, and that's a bad thing—a very bad thing.

Yes, this is her country, but she's young and I'm a fish out of water. I have no idea how to navigate through this desolate, snow covered terrain. Obviously, there is nothing like the equivalent of AAA. The wind keens around the corners of the house, reminding me that old man winter is hungry, and we look like fresh meat.

"What should we do?" she asks in a small voice.

"Well, for the next few minutes, we're not going to do anything. Then, we're going to take the Sherpa's coat because he won't need it, and we do. Staying warm is our number one priority for the next day or two. I'll take the Sherpa out and leave him in the snow so when he is found after the snow melts it will appear he got lost and died in the storm. When I come back, we'll figure out what we need to do next."

She pulls up her knees and hugs herself. The firelight dances on her cheeks making her look vulnerable, young and incredibly beautiful. Even as the Sherpa lies dead on the floor, the sight of her naked flashes through my mind, I can't help the lust rising inside me. My sick mind wants me to go over to the mattress, strip her naked and have sex with her in front of the fire. I push the terrible idea out of my mind. I never imagined I'd be the kind of man who'd think of screwing in front of the dead.

"I—I've never ..." she starts.

"I know," I tell her. "And the first time is the worst." I thought about my first dead body. I was eight. Anakin made me watch. I stand. "I better take him out."

"You'll do it alone?" she asks.

"Yeah, I'll do it alone."

"I don't mean to be a baby, but I, well, I ..."

"Don't worry about it. In fact, don't worry about anything. You may as well go to sleep."

"I have to pee, first," she says.

I laugh. "Yeah, there's that, and neither one of us wants to go outside. Here's how I see it. We can spend half the night filling up the toilet tank with snow and seeing how well it works ... or you can pee in the sink. It isn't like we're going to be washing dishes there."

She makes a face at the prospect. "But that would be rude to the people who own this house."

I scratch my jaw. Principles are postures taken by those that can afford it. When your very existence is on the line, you lose everything except the need to survive. "If I were you. I'd go for the sink. We can save the toilet for the other number."

She nods slowly. "All right. I'll go while you are out."

I haul the Sherpa's lifeless body up and throw him over my shoulder. Then I go out of the front door. The wind and snow assault me. I duck my head and take him far enough away from the house and lay him on the snow. Then I strip his coat off and look through it. I find a passport for the girl in his inside pocket. After I put it into my jacket pocket, I position his body into a fetal position so it looks as if he froze to death to the people who find him. That is, if the animals don't strip his flesh and move his bones away.

I turn away and start to retrace my steps back to shelter and Katya. My toes are already going numb, and my face feels half-frozen. It's amazing how quickly one loses heat. It is a relief to see the flickering orange light in the windows of the house. As I reach the side of the house, I can't help looking in.

Katya back on the mattress, hugging her calves, her back to the door, and her chin on her knees. She looks lost and scared.

I know death has placed a large, cold hand on her heart. It always does, because it's not the death of someone else that grabs us, it's our own death. Every time someone dies, we are reminded of our own mortality, and accepting that mortality is the hardest lesson a human has to learn. We're finite, and until we understand that, we'll waste our lives and chase the things that won't make any difference. I've seen death enough.

I push open the door and she turns to look at me. She says nothing as I join her on the mattress. I take the coat and put it around her.

"I don't—"

"Shh," I tell her. "It will keep you warm."

"Are you sure? It seems like desecration or something."

"He doesn't need it anymore." I don't touch her. That's not the right thing to do no matter how she looks underneath her clothes. We stare into the small fire. It's hardly hot enough to keep us warm, but it beats the hell out of the blizzard cold. We sit there for a minute before she puts her hand on mine.

"Thank you," she says with a smile, and that changes the air in the small space.

Suddenly, I can feel the heat from her body and smell her scent. Furious with myself, I stand hurriedly and walk to the fire. I add another log to it and look at our supply. We're going to need more. "I'm going to get more wood," I tell her. "When I kick the door, open it."

"I can go with you."

"No need. You'll just get cold."

"At least take the coat." She shrugs off the coat and holds it out to me.

"Wear it and stay warm. It won't fit me." With a smile, I head out.

The glow from the snow gives enough light for me to see my way. I look left and right, hoping to find the Sherpa's tracks from when he brought in the last load. I'm not that lucky. What I see could be anything. I turn right because right-handed people usually turn that way, and head around the house, slogging through the snow, looking for the wood pile. I have to go around three corners before I find the pile.

It's a good-sized pile. At least Katya and I aren't going to freeze to death. I pile as many as I can carry across my arms and slog on. I kick the door hard. She must have been waiting because the door opens immediately, and I push into the light and warmth. Not that much warmth, but better than the outside. I add my armload to the stock already on the floor and shake off the snow.

There is relief on her face as she watches me. Maybe she was thinking that I might not come back, that the cold and snow would do for me what a heart attack did for the Sherpa, and she would die here on her own, but even though I know her concern is motivated by selfish reasons, it feels right that she was waiting for me to return to her. "Go get warm," I tell her.

Katya goes to the end of the mattress and sits. I hang the coat over the chair to dry and I join her at the end of the mattress. I put my arm around her, and she rests her head on my shoulder. There's nothing sexual in the gesture. It is almost that of a frightened child seeking reassurance.

"We're not going to die here, are we?" she asks.

"Not a chance," I lie. Actually, I give us a fifty-fifty chance of surviving. People die in blizzards every winter, even smart people. I'm not so smart, and I wonder about her. We stare into the flames. I think of Detroit and Anakin, but my life there has taken on a dream-like quality. As if it was never real. Only this shelter and tiny fire and the head on my shoulders are true.

At this moment, I have no desire to go back. If there was a way to forage for food here, this would be my idea of paradise.

KATYA

The American is strong and capable. He handled the Sherpa in a way I didn't expect. And he retrieved more wood for us. They're not as dry as the first logs. The log he put in pops and hisses in the fire, but it's wood, and it gives off light and heat. That's what we need at the moment. His arm reassures me, but I can tell he isn't very confident that we'll survive. He hides his fears the best he can, but I'm Russian. I understand how nature and bad luck can kill a person. This is a harsh country.

As I look into the fire, I remember how he looks naked. I remember the sex. I remember having him in my mouth and … other places. A sudden fire ignites in my belly. I have had sex only once, but my body seems to crave it. It is a visceral thing, a body thing. My brain has no control over it. No reason, no rationality. I don't know how it happened, but the desire is always there.

It's almost an ache. Only a couple of days ago I knew nothing of what being with a man can feel like. I don't know if my presence affects him, but he moves suddenly. His eyes slide down and glance at my breasts. I know immediately what he's thinking about. I know he sees me naked. I have no idea if I look pleasing or not to him, but I know I'm in his brain, like his image is in mine.

There's nothing else to do on this godforsaken night.

He turns my chin and looks into my eyes. "Are you all right?"

His touch is tender, filled with concern. His eyes show a glow that I recognize. He is pretending he doesn't want it, but he's thinking of sex, both last night and tonight.

We're human. We dream of sex.

HUNTER

https://www.youtube.com/watch?v=
C_3d6GntKbk&index=89&
(Pillowtalk)

"I'm cold," she whispers, looking into my eyes.

Her face is pale, but there it is again. That thing between us. My heart pounds furiously within my chest. *Anakin. You owe him everything,* a voice whispers inside my head. It is just loud enough to keep my reasoning intact. This is Anakin's girl. Having sex with her again isn't going to solve anything. "I'll get some more wood," I say hoarsely, and start to stand.

She grabs both my wrists and pulls at them. "I don't need a bigger fire. I need *your* warmth."

I pull my wrists out of her grasp and walk towards the fire.

"Does my being close to you affect you *that* much?" she mocks softly.

I sit by the fire and pick up a stick to stoke it. Her eyes are on me. I know because I can feel her gaze piercing and bringing more heat than the crackling fire I was sitting right in front of.

Unable to utter a word, I just glare at the yellow flames as the moments tick by. The chill is gradually being chased away and in its place is an acute awareness of her. It is so strong I begin to sweat. It is only when I catch her in my peripheral vision as she begins to fall gently back onto the mattress, that I can no longer hold back. I turn to watch.

I can see her body trembling. My Princess turns her head and looks at me. I swallow the stone in my throat. Then she opens her mouth and calls to me. It was almost soundless, but I can feel it reverberate through me like a body of water disturbed by a stone skipping on its surface. "Hunter."

Instantly, I go to her.

Sitting on the mattress, I pick her up and pull her into my arms. She truly is trembling and I feel a painful remorse wash through me as I link my fingers with hers. I wonder how she could be so cold.

"You're cruel," she whispers to me as her eyes shut.

I watch her angelic face, my chest tight. How could she have such an effect over me? Her soft pink mouth parts and I can't stop myself. I'm only a man. I lower my head and take her lips in a soft kiss. The contact thrusts a painful dose of desire straight to my cock.

She kisses me back, slowly, purposefully, and I can almost

convince myself that all she's looking for is as much heat from me as is possible. Her hands come around my neck as she deepens the kiss. I can still remember how shy and tentative her mouth was only a day ago. She pulls away and in the next moment, she is straddling my hips and my back is slammed to the floor. With her hands to my shoulders she pins me in place and begins to gyrate her hips, rubbing her pussy against my already swollen dick.

"Katya," I snarl warningly, but she squirms her hips and her wetness soaks through our clothes. I take a shuddering breath. God, this woman is a natural seductress who has taken to sex like a duck to water. And I need her. I need her so fucking bad, my head feels like it is going to damn well explode if I don't have her.

"We need this for warmth," she says. "You can console yourself with that."

I grab both her arms and roll her to the mattress. She gasps with surprise as we change positions and I pin her arms high above her head, making her breasts jut out.

"You're hurting me," she breathes.

I know that is a lie, but my hold on her hands loosens, and quick as a flash she reaches up to press her cold nose to mine, her eyes so close that I can make out the streaks of gold in her irises. She doesn't move and neither do I.

"I'm really cold Hunter" she whispers, and her breath, so warm and direct on my skin is like an aphrodisiac.

She is right. The damage is done. We're already in trouble. What difference would it make if we have sex again? I part her lips with mine and slip my tongue into her mouth. The taste of her is clean and warm and haunting.

It takes me past reason.

With my hand around her neck, I hold her in place and savor the dance of my tongue against hers. She becomes more fervent as I trace kisses along her jaw and down her neck to the rapid beating of her pulse. I lick it like an animal and she starts to tear her clothes off her body.

"You'll be too cold," I caution.

"You're all the warmth I need," she says, lifting her body so she can unhook her bra and expose her goose-pimpled breasts. Then she pulls off her panties and lies under me, naked.

Pulling off my sweater, I cover one breast in my warm hand and suck the other pink-tipped, taut nipple into my mouth. With frenzied movements, she begins to tear at the button of my jeans and pulls down the zipper.

I allow her to take the reins. She urges me onto my back. I lay back and watch as she slides my jeans and briefs off to expose my hard cock.

Holding the thick shaft adoringly in her hands my beautiful Princess licks down it until she has my balls in her mouth. I shut my eyes, ecstasy melting my insides. Soon, her wet warm mouth covers the mushroom head and she sucks long and slow. I groan with the exquisite pleasure. Her hands close around my shaft and up and down she goes, her tongue lapping up whatever pre-cum that spills out of me.

I've been blown countless times like this in the past, but with Katya it seems as if my cock was made specifically for her mouth. "Don't stop ... *fuck*," I hear myself say to her. The scrape of her teeth down the thickly veined sensitive flesh, brings me to the edge of a mindless explosion. "Finish me off," I command, unable to contain myself any longer.

Her small hand tightens around my dick and she sucks for all she is worth.

"Ah, Katya." I come with the roar of a beast, hot spurts of semen shooting straight into her mouth and down her throat. She laps it all up like a starving woman. I go over the edge and the pleasure is so intense it feels as if my body, my bones, my being, is disintegrating into nothing.

When I come back down to earth, I grab her around the ribs and pull her up to me. The smile on her face is heart stopping. I taste myself on her lips as I kiss her. She wraps her arms around either side of my head and her chest flattens against mine as the kiss deepens. My hands reach for her ass to grind her into me.

Time stops while we kiss. Slowly, my body recognizes that primitive, insatiable need to be inside her again. Curling my hands around her thighs, I open them and lift her hips up over my erect cock. "I'm going in bare," I tell her.

"I want you to. If we die in this crazy place at least I will have experienced your cock shooting its seed into my belly."

She fists my dick as I impale her on it. She is so goddamn tight, so hot, so soft, her pretty cunt greedily gripping me, urging me deeper and deeper until I can go no further.

With her hands on my chest she shuts her eyes and savors it all. Then she begins to move, riding me, slowly and then hard ... She slams her body down on me again and again. Our mating is violent and desperate. We are the only two people left in the world. Outside the blizzard continues. Tomorrow we could be dead. Today we are driving each other insane with pleasure.

With her hands on my chest, she fucks me, her breasts bouncing with her furious moves until every nerve in my body grows taut with anticipation for the coming release.

She explodes just before I do, her hips jerking at the force and intensity of her climax. "Hunter," she cries again and again even while I explode inside her. Her entire body is still trembling as she collapses on me.

You'll be the death of me, is all I can think.

KATYA

https://www.youtube.com/watch?v=paXOkGMyG8M&list
-I can see a rainbow-

Hunter kisses me and I kiss him back. I love kissing him. I like his lips which feel smooth. I like his tongue which licks at mine. But mostly, I love the clean taste of him. My friends have talked about the boys they kiss. Boys who are aggressive and tactless, boys who treat kissing as a necessary evil, boys whose tongues are little, hungry things that they force on their girlfriends.

As I kiss him, I try to remember what my friends have said, what seems to make boys happy, what a good kiss is made of. But I can't remember. I can only feel his lips and tongue and the movements that seem right no matter what he does. It all feels right. I almost think I need it. Death howls just outside the door, but this … this is life. This is what I was born to do. He cannot know how good he tastes, how warm he makes me. Soon, I will not need the fire. I will burn bright, like a candle. I will consume myself.

He pauses and pulls back, his face is serious.

I sense his need, his desire. It matches mine, I think.

"Cold?" he asks.

I shake my head. I wouldn't admit it even if I were cold. He touches me, and his touch is gentle, smooth. He doesn't wish to cause any damage, to use me too much. Maybe it is because he thinks that would make it easy for Anakin to pronounce me impure. He spreads my legs, once again he bends down and licks me. When he first did it last night, I could hardly believe what he was doing. I didn't believe it until I felt his tongue lick me.

My body shivers with pleasure.

I close my eyes and concentrate on what he's doing, what his tongue is doing. It's so delicious and like nothing I've ever felt before. He licks and probes and gently spreads me. It's like some sort of creature that is curious, attentive, warm and wet. I can feel it touch me in places I've never been touched before.

As his tongue wiggles and licks, I burn brighter. I feel need. My hips wish to move. My body wishes to accept and capture that little creature that teases me. A spasm ripples through my tummy. Quickly, he finds spots that are more sensitive than I would have believed until I met him.

Finally, his tongue lands on the thing I never knew I had. The something that is incredibly sensitive, incredibly hungry. It pulsates with heat and need. He seems to know how it works, how it quivers when he licks it, how it throbs when his tongue leaves it. I was afraid during my first orgasm. I thought I was dying. No one told me it would be like that. Now that I know how it feels, I want it. I want it in a way I thought I would never want anything.

He pauses and looks at me. "Like that?" he asks.

I clutch his head. "Don't stop."

Hunter returns to satisfying my need. He licks again, and my heart starts beating faster as my blood pounds through my body. His tongue does things to me that are mysteries. He presses his tongue down on me, and I gasp. I want too much to respond, to arch, drive and push, but I don't. I will let him tend to me. I will let him push me higher. I will let him make me burn with sheer heat.

I moan.

His hands grab my thighs, and his tongue pumps in and out, like a tiny piston. I feel a huge beast inside me, a huge, powerful thing that strains at the chains that hold it in place. The first time I had been a bit frightened as I never knew there was this thing inside me. Something held in place like a fly in a spider's web. It wants life. It wants to explode. It actually feels as if it breaks its manacles, it will consume me.

"Yesssssssssss," I hiss. He is so good at this.

I feel the chains slipping.

His tongue presses again.

The beast inside thrashes and roars, and then it happens.

My brain shuts down. The thing inside rushes through my body, through my veins, my muscles, my bones. It is like an army of feeling, thousands of little soldiers that leap upon every nerve in my body, prodding and pricking, sending a billion flashing signals to my brain. I become nothing more than a bundle of feeling, a huge, hot bundle of sheer joy. It is immediate and overwhelming. I am lost. All my thoughts are gone. I become one with the universe. My mouth opens.

And I scream.

HUNTER

https://www.youtube.com/watch?v=gb-B3lsgEfA
(It's A Man's World)

When she screams, I press my tongue on her clit and keep it there to extend her orgasm. To my surprise it doesn't just extend her climax it gives her multiple orgasms. Fascinated, I watch her have the most enthralling experience of her life.

When it is finally over, I stop and crouch over her. She smiles at me dreamily. I smile back.

"That—that was sooooo amazing," she whispers. "I think I am addicted to sex now."

I hide a smile at her innocence. "None of us have any idea until we try it. Once we do, we want it all the time."

"Yes, yes, again and again," she says eagerly.

I pick up her panties and hand them to her. "Get dressed. We need to keep warm."

She slides on her panties as I retrieve her jeans. "Thank you," she says. "I want you to know that you touched me deeply."

I pull on my jeans and sweater quickly. I don't want her stupid gratitude. The more time I spend with her the more I like her and that pisses me off. Why couldn't she be a whiny brat or a self-obsessed selfie addict?

"You know, I was thinking that perhaps we will not get out of this. But after tonight, I think I might be able to die in peace. I won't have to haunt the planet looking for something I had never experienced."

I whirl around to face her. "We *are* going to get through this. Things look and sound bad tonight, but the morning will come. When it does, we will assess our position and make plans. I'm not going to die in some crummy house in the middle of Russia. That isn't my fate. And if it's not mine, it's not yours either. Now, we should probably sleep."

I watch her fasten her jeans, and I can't stop the lust that floods my body again. I could take her right now, but I won't. The closer I get to her the harder it will be to hand her over to Anakin. Just the thought is already sticking like a claw in my gut. I get the Sherpa's coat and cover her.

She smiles at me innocently.

It makes me feel like a heel. I don't know what Anakin has done to the other girls and what plans he has for her, but they can't be good. I add another log to the fire, and I think perhaps we have enough for the night, but not enough for tomorrow. I push tomorrow out of my mind. I will face those problems when they arise. I bundle up and lie down next to her.

She moves closer to me and lifts the coat. "We share," she says.

I nod and move against her, under the coat. Her heat radiates through me. I remember her orgasm. Then I have the wild and totally unrealistic thought that maybe I could buy her from Anakin. I have some money saved. I would give it all to him if he would sell her to me. The idea is so stupid it makes my eyes snap open. I stare into the fire blankly. The flames remind me that we all burn in the end. Maybe Katya and I will burn out quicker than most people.

I close my eyes and tell myself to sleep. In the morning, in the morning ...

I wake up freezing. A glance at the fire shows me there are only a few glowing embers left. There's light in the room, so it's after daybreak. I move and Katya rolls away, hugging the coat tighter. I scoot across the cold floor to the stack of wood and add a log to the fire. Then, I grab another log and stoke the embers. They're hot enough I think to start the log burning. I hope so. The log in my hand is the last log in the house. I need to get more, but I'll wait till she wakes. I want to see her when she first opens her eyes.

I go to the window and look out. The wind has diminished as has the snow. The glass is too dirty and frosty to see much. I don't need to see much to know this is a bad spot to be in, very bad. We're going to get out today if we can. There's absolutely no reason to stay if the weather cooperates. We will never be stronger than we are right now, never warmer, never more able to survive. Waiting for someone to rescue us is insane. Every hour does little but take a bit more of our energy.

I grab some glasses and fill them from the pump. I carry the glasses three at a time to the bathroom and fill the toilet tank. I'm not sure why I'm doing this. I'm not usually so solicitous towards the women I sleep with. I suppose I want to give her some privacy. It's not much. In fact, it's a tiny thing, but that's the best I can do for her.

As I refill the toilet, I think about the night before, her orgasm. In a way, it was a stupid thing to do. It siphoned off a lot of her precious energy. Once the tank is nearly full, I go outside and relieve myself. It is so cold my urine becomes yellow ice as soon as it hits the ground.

By the time I come back in, she's awake. She smiles at me, the sweetest, brightest, most enchanting smile ever. No one would imagine that she is stuck in a cold hut in the middle of nowhere with death staring her in the face. Funny thing is I smile back. A smile that feels as if it is flowing from my heart.

"I've filled the toilet tank," I tell her. "You can use it."

Her eyes shine. "You filled it for me?"

"Yeah. I decided to fertilize the grounds."

She laughs, and it's a good strong laugh. The kind of laugh you wouldn't expect from such a beautiful face. I could learn to love her laugh. I could learn to love it until Anakin shoots me in the face.

I tell myself not to love the laugh too much.

126

HUNTER

On her way to the toilet she gives me a kiss, just a little
kiss, but it's enough. It says all that needs to be said.
She had a good night, and now she will join me in the business of getting us out of this mess. Even though my tongue
has licked and sucked every inch of her, she closes the bathroom door modestly.

For a few moments, I stand there staring at the closed door,
then I open the front door and face a world of white.

The snow has covered everything, and there is no trace of
the tracks we made yesterday. In the distance, I think I can
see the Ford Explorer. It's another lump in the snow. Beyond
that is the road, although I can see from here that it hasn't
been plowed or cleared. That's not encouraging, but it is
what it is. I look at the sky, and the light gray clouds are thin-
ning. The sun will come out soon. At least, I think it will, but
it will not have much heat. Zipping my jacket against the icy
wind, I leave the porch to fetch wood.

The snow is up to my knees, but it's not wet and heavy and

that's a good thing. Slogging through wet snow would be brutal. The light stuff will be bad enough. I grab enough logs to get us through the morning because that's as long as I think we should stay. The road is our only way out, and we have to reach it early in the day.

It's a desperate, mad idea, but it's the only one I've got. If we don't get picked up, we'll face another night in the cold, and there's no guarantee we'll find any more shelter. Alone in the dark and cold with no fire, we're facing almost certain death. If we huddle together, we might be able to stay warm. But waiting another day will only make us weaker and I can't believe we won't come across another human being on the road all day long.

Inside, I'm happy to see I haven't managed to kill the fire yet. It is burning brightly. Katya comes out of the bathroom, and I can tell that she's done something to her hair, smoothed it out and combed it so it hangs around her breasts. And just like that … my cock starts straining in my pants. I turn away from her. The last thing we need is to waste any time having sex.

"How are you?" I ask putting more logs onto the fire.

"Fine," she answers. "You?"

"As good as it gets. Have a seat, we need to plan how we're going to get out of this."

She sits on the mattress, and I settle down opposite her. I want to take her hand, but I don't. "Here's how I see things. The snow covered over every sign that we're here. Someone might see the smoke from the chimney, but there's no guarantee of that, and even if they do, they'll hardly think it strange. No one is looking for us because we haven't called anyone. Your parents won't come looking because you're on your way to America. The Sherpa's family might start looking for him in a day or two, but that's not guaranteed either. He might not even have a family. Our phones won't work. In short, we're on our own. Any rescue attempt won't happen for days if ever. They might not even find the vehicle before spring."

"So, you're thinking we should walk out?" she asks.

I nod. "I know it sounds crazy, but I don't see any way around it. Every day we wait, we'll grow a little weaker. It will get harder. We have plenty of water and there's enough wood for another two or three days, but we don't have food. I don't see anything moving out there, and even if I could, I don't have anything to hunt them with."

"What about the Sherpa?"

My eyes widen. "I know people in dire straits will eat anything they can find, but we're not going cannibal just yet."

She shakes her head. "What I mean is ... are we going to leave him here?"

"We don't have much choice. I'm a foreigner and I don't want any trouble. When we get back to the States, you can send a note to the embassy and explain what happened." I don't tell her that I've been bred to keep a safe distance from the police. Under no circumstances am I going to them for help.

"I understand," she says.

"So, we're going to be leaving soon. Once we're on the move, we won't talk unless we have to. We'll get to the road and we'll walk it until someone picks us up. I can't see how anyone would drive on and leave us to die out here. When we're picked up, you will tell them that we went into the ditch during the storm. We found a little house to stay in, but our vehicle is out of commission. We won't mention the Sherpa, OK?"

She nods.

"And when we get to a town, we'll get a ride on a train or bus or something. I don't think I can rent a car."

"I can't either."

"If we're lucky, we'll be well out of Russia before the Sherpa is found. I don't know about you, but that's fine with me."

"Actually, me too."

"Good, so we'll leave as soon as we've had something to drink. People dehydrate in the cold just like they do in the heat."

She squeezes my hand. "You're not sure we'll make it, are you?"

I don't tell her that I don't like our odds. I keep that to myself. "I won't lie to you. People die in the cold all the time, but if we can hike the road, we have a good chance. Better than staying here."

"We could make a sign or something."

"We could spell out HELP or something, but it could snow again later and it would take a plane to find the message. I don't know how many flights go over or how observant their pilots are. If we didn't have a road, I'd go for it. But we have a road."

"I am ready to go with you."

"Drink some water."

I watch her tip her head back and chug down two whole glasses of water. I'm glad she's game for the try. I look around the room. I'll kill the fire when we leave. I'd hate to burn down the house. I pull out my phone and turn it off. Draining the battery by trying to find a connection won't do us any good. "Wear the Sherpa's coat over yours, and you'll be that much warmer."

She nods and takes the coat.

I go to the fireplace and move the logs apart. They might burn for a while, but not for long. I take some water from the sink and douse the embers. I hate to see a good fire die. Fire is a good thing. "Ready?" I ask.

"Yes."

"I'll lead. You follow in my footprints, got it?"

She nods nervously.

"This is adventure," I tell her. "This is what keeps us alive. We'll make it."

She presses her lips and nods again.

I lead us out of the house and wait till she is out before I close the door. Without wasting time, I step off the porch and turn for the road. At that moment the clouds part, and a ray of sunlight hits the bright snow, almost blinding me. Maybe I'm an idiot for going out like this, but then, I don't have much choice. It's either be an idiot or hang around and starve to death. In my life, I've always tried to be the doer, not the one that things are done to. It seems to work for me.

A few yards away, I feel her touch my shoulder, and I turn to look at her.

She points with her hand. "Is that Sherpa over there?"

I glance over at the lump in the snow. His bright blue scarf had been disturbed by the wind and it was blowing like a flag. Almost as if calling to us. I stared at it. He was a good Sherpa while he lasted. I have no doubts about his ability. He did what he could. Too bad he had to die in that shelter.

"Shouldn't we say a prayer for him?" Katya asks.

We don't have time, but he's dead and she wants him to have a sendoff. "Fine," I say moving in the direction of his waving scarf. We stand in front of the Sherpa shaped lump of snow. "Go on then," I encourage.

"Dear God," she begins. "Please take this man's soul into heaven. I have no idea if he deserves it, but he did his best by us, and that counts for something. Amen." She makes the sign of the cross.

I've never had the time for religion. My take on God is simple. If there was a kind God above and we were all his children, he would never have allowed what happened to me to go on year after year. He would never allow men like Anakin to lord over men like Mooch.

She looks up at me. "It is a good thing we said our prayers for him."

I shrug. "You did."

"Don't you believe in God?" she asks curiously.

"Nah."

"But if you don't believe in God where will you go after you die?"

I laugh bitterly. "Hell, maybe."

Before she can say anything else I turn away. This is going to be a very hard slog and we better get on.

KATYA

https://www.youtube.com/watch?v=
ClU3fctbGls&index=145&

I follow in his footsteps, literally.

His legs are longer than mine so his stride is long, but I can manage. And following is far better than leading. In snow this deep, leading is very hard work. The cold makes my nose tingle and run, but the extra coat keeps me warm. I won't freeze to death just yet.

The walk reminds me of when I was small, a child sent to school. Many days I had to walk, and in the winter, it was always a freezing cold walk, mostly in the snow. I was never afraid then. There were houses, buildings and cars, and the cold was merely an inconvenience, not deadly. I used to sing even though I was never a good singer. It was easier to walk if one had a rhythm. The steps were the tempo.

How many times did I hear the same song in my head? I hear it now. But the tempo is too fast. This is slow, methodical. I look up, and he has moved a little bit ahead. I want to tell him that I think he's walking too fast. He will wear out, and then, he will quit. There is a science to walking in the cold. Moving too fast, breathing too hard, the lungs will be damaged. If he fails, we will both die.

This thought almost makes me sick.

Hunter gave me the best gift I ever received. He is the reason we're still alive. He's done all the right things. But while I am grateful I don't fully trust him. I know he still plans to hand me over to Anakin. I suppose the harsh truth is he shouldn't trust me either because the first opportunity I get, I plan to escape. He's a foreigner here. He will never be able to find me. I feel bad for what Anakin will do to him, but he doesn't have to go back to him. He could run away too. If he doesn't, it's his business. I have to think of my poor parents and my sister. They'll need money from me. I step into the next footprint.

How much farther?

I shield my eyes the best I can and look up. The sun reflecting off the snow is brutal. It is white-white, blinding. Still, I do what I have to do. I follow. And I don't talk because as Hunter said that takes energy. I already feel that I don't have enough. The last time I ate was a slice of birthday cake and my stomach is growling like crazy at the thought of food. To take my mind off the hunger pangs, I keep my head down and savor the memory of last night's orgasm.

In a way, dying in the cold would be the perfect solution. I will not be beaten because I am no longer a virgin. I will not be sold into slavery. I will not join a harem in some far away land, but I don't want to die. I'm only eighteen. I want to escape and find a way to help my family. The money that they have been getting from Anakin is going to stop as soon as he finds out I became a runner. Adventure, that's what the American calls this. He sees adventure.

Suddenly, I see him running ahead of me.

What?

Protecting my eyes with my hands I see why. A truck is coming along the road, and he is trying to reach the road before the truck passes. He moves quickly, and then, he falls. I chase, and now his steps are too far apart for me. I can't reach every one of them, which slows me. I watch as he gets up and runs, but he's limping now.

He hurt his leg in the fall.

It's clear he's not going to make it. Even as I watch, the truck passes without slowing. He waves and shouts, but the truck is gone. If they saw him, they ignored him. He stands, waving far longer than he should. They're gone. We're still here, and now he's hurt. I hope he isn't hurt badly.

The truck is no more when he limps onto the road. He is slower than before. He has used a lot of energy, precious energy.

I follow. I lower my head and concentrate on his steps. If he stepped in a hole, I don't want to repeat his fall.

I concentrate on the steps, the snow. I reach the place where he fell, and I see the hole he stepped into. I avoid the hole and keep going. I hope Hunter hasn't hurt himself too badly. If there isn't a ride, we will have a long walk. If he's hurt …

There is a sharp pain in my chest. I don't complete the thought. Of course, he's not hurt.

He's waiting for me on the snow covered road. It's been plowed, but it's still snow covered. It will be a much easier walk, but I see nothing in either direction.

"Are you all right?" I ask.

"Yeah, I'm fine. Stupid, fucking hole," he curses. "And for what? I missed the truck anyway."

"It was worth the try."

"Maybe. Which way?"

I look in both directions. Everything looks the same. "I have no idea which way we are going."

"I don't know either," he says. "And I have no idea if we're closer to the town we are going to, or to the town we left." He holds his hand up to his eyes and squints into the distance. "That's the car, I think. That means we were going that way." He points in the opposite direction.

"I think so too. We can walk side by side if you want. We just need to keep an eye out for vehicles. We don't want to get run over."

"I agree. Russians are maniacs on the road."

Walking single file doesn't appeal to me. This will be boring enough the way it is.

"Let's go." He walks on my left, putting me closest to the side of the road.

Now that he's hurt, I find it easy to keep up with him. "What did you hurt?" I ask.

"Ankle. Just a little twist. Luckily, it's too cold for the thing to swell much."

"Painful?"

"I've had worse."

I remember his little speech about not talking, so I don't ask any more questions. We walk in silence, and I let my mind wander. The sun's brightness makes me look down at my feet. There is something to be said for not looking too far ahead. If you don't look, you don't wonder when you're going to reach that next rise.

KATYA

I know something about this area of Russia. There are no mountains here, no great forests. There are patches of woods here and there, rolling hills, and flat plains now covered in snow. From what I remember from school, this is a fertile and lonely farm country. In fact, I can't see a house or anything, and I can easily see a kilometer or two. Of course, there could be a town or village over the next hill. We can't know. We can only walk.

"What was your favorite subject in school?" he asks.

"I thought we weren't going to talk."

"We have to do something to kill the boredom. Otherwise, we'll go crazy out here. It's either talk, or sing, and you don't want to hear me sing."

I laugh. "I don't want to sing either." I glance over, and I spot a hint of pain in his face, a bit of grimace. He's hurt worse than he lets on. "I liked school," I admit. "I wasn't the smartest girl in the class, but I was smart enough and my teachers liked me. Math wasn't my best subject. I preferred literature. I read every book I could. When I was reading, I didn't hear my parents arguing. I didn't feel so hungry either. I was someone else, someone that everyone loved or respected. I remember long afternoons in my room with a book and some tea. My favorites were mysteries. I loved mysteries. I still do. I love how detectives figure out everything, even when I couldn't. Everything changed for my family when I was twelve and I joined the program."

"Program?"

I glance sideways at him. He really doesn't know anything. "The program is when a girl is chosen by Anakin to come to America."

He looks astonished. "You were picked when you were twelve?"

"Yes. We all are. Once I was enrolled into the program, my parents were given money and our lives improved greatly. A teacher came two times a week to teach me English."

The wind blows hard but not as hard as last night. It's cold, and I know we can't last a night in this wind, even if we can keep walking. How many kilometers can I walk? I'm not sure, but I guess perhaps twenty or thirty. No, that's probably too many in the snow, I don't think I can do more than fifteen. "What about you? Did you like school?"

"I didn't go to school."

"What? Don't all Americans have to go to school?"

He winces. "I guess they do, but I didn't."

"Why not?"

"It's a long story."

"Well, I've got time," I say softly.

"I guess it's because I was sold to Anakin when I was four years old and he didn't think school was what I needed."

I'm so shocked I stop walking and stare at him in astonishment.

He stops too.

We stare at each other.

I take a deep breath. "Hunter, I'm sorry. I'm really sorry."

He shrugs. "Don't be. I would probably have hated school. Besides, I liked hanging around on the corner." He starts walking again.

I follow him "The corner?"

"That's what we call the streets. You go out and be with wise guys, criminals. If they take a shine to you, they teach you what's going on."

"What did they teach you?"

"How to use a gun, how to avoid the cops, how to deal drugs, how to hold up a liquor store. You can learn a lot on the corner."

"Did the police catch you?"

"Couple times. Nothing I couldn't chisel down."

"Chisel down?"

"In America, they always charge you with the worst crime they can. So, there's always room for a lesser crime. You get caught for dealing drugs, and they charge you with a big felony. But if you're not an asshole, they'll chisel it down to possession only. Then, you pay some money. In my case, Anakin does and you don't go to prison. It's a game. The prosecutor gets a conviction without much work, and I get to go back to the corner and carry on working for Anakin."

"So you enjoy working for Anakin?" I say slowly.

"I don't know anything else," he says simply.

I watch him intently. "Have you ever killed anyone, Hunter?"

He hesitates, and I think I already know the truth. He will probably lie, but I will know. He has killed. That changes him a little in my eyes. I have never met a killer before.

"I'll tell you the truth. I've killed. Mostly, I don't even need a gun. I'm strong and pretty good with my hands."

"Hands?"

"I can handle myself in a fight. Comes in handy cause you don't want to kill someone. And if you're carrying a gun, the cops don't like it. They charge you with more crimes."

"That you can chisel down," I finish for him.

"Yeah." He grins. "There's that."

"When I was five, I wanted to be a ballerina," I tell him. "I think every active girl in Russia wants to be a ballerina or a gymnast. That dream only lasted until I understood my parents weren't rich enough to pay for lessons."

We reach the top of the rise and we can see a good way off. Far away, I spot a town, some decent sized buildings or houses. Or it could be just something in the air, some sort of mirage. I can't be sure.

"See it?" he asks.

"Yes," I answer. "A town."

"How far?"

"I don't know. A long walk."

"Yeah, I figured that."

We start down the hill, and I wish we were closer. Hunter isn't doing all that well. His limp is getting worse and I can hear the pain in his voice. It's funny how the voice changes when there's pain involved.

"Where do you live in Detroit?" I ask, hoping to take his mind off his pain.

"On the north side."

"I'm glad it was you Anakin sent to pick me up," I say.

"It's not over yet," he mutters.

I know that. Anakin sent him to bring me back. If he doesn't do that, he's in trouble. Do I care if he goes back and Anakin hurts him? Yes, I do. I don't want him to get hurt. Before we leave Russia, I will try to convince him to run away with me. I've heard that America is rich, so rich anyone can live like a king. Florida, I think we should run away to Florida together.

"No matter what happens, I'm glad it was you," I say softly.

We hear the vehicle before we see it. It's coming from behind, so we move to the side of the road and hold up our hands. We need the ride if we can get it. It's a large truck, and it slows as soon as it sees us. We must look awful. They pass us and stop. We walk to the vehicle as a man climbs out and faces us. He doesn't smile.

"What are you doing out here?" he asks in Russian.

"Our car broke down. We barely made it to the road."

He opens the rear door. "Get in, get in. This is no day to be out for a walk."

We slide into the backseat and the driver eyes me in the mirror. I don't know how much he can see since I am well bundled. The American simply sits, as if he doesn't know anything. The other man climbs into the front, and the truck starts off.

"I'm Dimitri," the driver says.

"And I'm Vasili," the other man says.

"I'm Katya," I tell them. "And he's Igor."

Vasili looks sharply at Hunter. "What's wrong with him?"

"He's deaf." I poke Hunter and make some hand signals. It's nonsense, but I don't think the men up front can tell.

Hunter signs back with just as much gibberish.

"You related?" Vasili asks, his eyes sliding over my uncovered hair.

"He's my cousin," I reply. "I was taking him to Moscow because they might be able to do something for his hearing."

"It was certainly a bad storm last night. How did you survive?"

"We found a vacant house and managed to build a fire."

"Then, you must be hungry. Dimitri, they're hungry. We must feed our guests."

"There's no need," I say quickly. "We simply need to get to a rail station."

"We'll get you there. After we stop. What kind of people would we be if we sent you off hungry?"

I don't like the sound of them, but I know better than to protest too much. I glance at Hunter who frowns at me. Their accents are thick, but I think he still understood the gist of our conversation. His eyes flash when the truck takes a side road that has been plowed, but is narrow and winding.

I feel the first stirrings of fear. Hunter is hurt and without food and all the walking we did, would be no match for these two brutish country men. No one knows where we are, and if we disappear, no one will ever know. They'll feed us to the hogs or something. I have heard stories about men like Dimitri and Vasili.

We're not on the road very long before we come upon a little drive that leads to a small house and two barns. Dimitri drives past the house and into one of the barns. There are some stalls, but no animals. He kills the engine and we all get out.

I manage to make eye contact with Hunter whose look says he's aware of the situation, play along.

"We'll have the food right away," Vasili says cheerfully.

Out of the truck, I notice just how big Dimitri is. He's a giant, dwarfing Vasili and at least a few inches taller than Hunter. He leers at me and I turn away. I don't want him to get the idea that I am not a modest woman, but I'm afraid he already has ideas about me. If only I had thought to cover my hair this morning instead of leaving it loose, because I wanted Hunter to admire it.

Vasili leads us into the house while Dimitri appears to guard the rear. I look around desperately, but there isn't anyone else around. It's just me, Hunter and the two brutes. I feel my body tighten warningly.

The house could have been nice if it wasn't so dirty and stinky. There's trash all about; clothes are draped over the furniture. It smells of stale food and old sweat. There's a table and chairs and a sink filled with dirty pans and dishes. These two live like pigs, and hungry pigs can be dangerous. On the walls hang paddles with sports team logos. They are fans.

"Sit down, sit down," Vasili invites, waving towards the table.

Hunter takes off his coat and sits. I start to move forward, and I take one step before Dimitri grabs my arm. He's incredibly strong. I'm going nowhere.

"I want to talk to you," Dimitri says.

He smells like a goat and I feel my stomach contract with fear, but I know I can't protest. He can crush me and I'm certain he can crush Hunter. "I have to stay with my cousin," I say. "He gets scared when people don't understand him."

"Vasili will take care of your cousin. Right, Vasili?"

Vasili seats Hunter at the table, facing away from me. They're separating us on purpose.

Hunter, when he isn't weakened with hunger and hurt would

definitely be strong enough to handle Vasili, but Dimitri is another matter.

"I'll take care of him," Vasili answers.

"I'm hungry," I tell Dimitri. "I need to eat."

He grins. "I'll give you a nice big sausage to eat. You like sausages no? A nice girl like you." He jerks me toward a door, a bedroom no doubt.

"Please," I say. "Don't do this."

"You're going to love it. And I guarantee to hurt you."

"RAPE!" I yell in English.

"What is this?" Dimitri asks, frowning.

"Let me be," I say in Russian. "You are a pig."

"I will show you what a pig is like." He picks me off the floor as easily as he would lift a kitten and carries me toward the bedroom.

"RAPE!" I yell again, kicking and screaming.

HUNTER

All the hairs on my neck and back are standing and the muscles of my thighs are twitching to jump up and strangle the bastard who had dared to touch my Princess, but I have enough sense to know that would be the death of both of us. The only advantage I might have is that I'm supposed to be the deaf, idiot savant cousin. I don't have a lot of time though to make my move.

The giant will not just rape her he will beat the shit out of her. I know men like him. They like to inflict pain. Makes them feel good. Makes them get hard. Making a girl scream and beg is how they get their rocks off. The giant will kill the girl when he and this other fool in front of me are done with her. Then me. I knew that from the moment they picked us up. And I've been ready for it ever since.

Vasili pretends to prepare food. He pulls a dirty plate, a fork, and a butter knife from the sink and places them in front of me. Keeping my mouth slightly open I just look at him with a dense expression. He gives me a sly smile and makes sure to show me how he's going to feed me. Then he goes to the small unbelievably stained fridge and opens the door. While his back is to me I glance around quickly. There is a big, sharp knife on the counter, and I think it will serve.

I grip the butter knife and move.

Vasili doesn't hear me until I punch him in the kidney hard. He grunts in shock and pain then falls forward towards the open fridge. In a flash, I grab his chin and jerk back his head. The butter knife is dull, but it's sharp enough if I find the right medium to stick it in. I jam it into his eye while I hold his mouth together. His scream comes out muffled and incoherent. The other eye is wide and rolling around wildly in its socket. He's not small and the adrenaline is beginning to kick in. He'll soon be hard to handle even with a knife in his eye.

I jerk him to the counter and grab the sharp knife. Pulling hard on his chin, I expose his white neck. The technique is a little messy, but it's simple, quick, and effective. I stab the knife into his neck and rip it out towards the front. I catch the artery and blood spurts out in a red fountain. Since I've cut his windpipe too, he won't' be able to warn the giant, which is a good thing. I need all the surprise I can get. I drop him and he flops on the floor, still grabbing his throat. He'll be dead in minutes if not seconds.

I don't need to wait to be sure.

I limp to the door and hesitate. I tighten my grip on the bloody knife and take a deep breath. I hope I'm lucky.

I open the door soundlessly.

The giant has his back to me. His pants are around his ankles and he's standing in front of a bed. His body is so big I cannot see Katya, but it is clear he has thrown her on it and has done something that has silenced her, but I'm pretty certain she's still alive.

This is about as good as it gets for me and Katya. I cross the room as fast as I can and stab the giant in the back. I don't think I hit anything vital, a lung maybe, but that's not going to stop this beast.

The giant roars and whirls around. He is surprisingly fast for a man of his size. I head-butt him full on the forehead with all my might. With his pants around his ankles he's not stable, his arms flail and he hits the floor with a loud thump. I can't take the time to look at Katya. If I can't take care of the giant, it won't make any difference.

With the knife gripped in my right hand I drop to one knee.

The giant must think I'm going for his hard prick, because his hands go there to protect himself. But I'm not going for that. I want his hairy, unprotected thigh. I slash it fast and deep. I hit pay dirt when I nick his femoral artery. Dark red blood pumps out. I try to jump back, but I'm not quick enough.

He snags my pants.

I try to get away, and I might have had a chance if my ankle wasn't beat up. His grip is too strong and I know he's going to win this little battle. I toss away the knife because I have no fantasies about keeping it from him if he gets me. And he's going to get me.

That's a scary prospect.

I jerk away to prime him and then I spin and land both knees on his chest, hoping to drive out his breath. It doesn't work. It hurts him, but it doesn't stop him. He grabs my throat with one hand and starts to squeeze. I grab his hand with both of mine, but I don't stand much chance of breaking his grip. Even as he bleeds out, he has enough strength to crush my throat and kill me. He looks me in the eye and smiles. He knows he's going to kill me, even if he dies doing it.

I glare at him. We'll die together.

The edge of a wooden paddle he must have been intending to use on Katya hits the giant in the middle of his broad face, breaking his nose, and causing blood to gush out. Dazed, his grip relaxes a bit, and I work to pry off his fingers.

No dice.

I look up as Katya hammers the giant again with that paddle, this time right on his forehead. The skin there splits and blood flows out. His grip relaxes still more—but not enough. My breathing is easier. I grab his thumb and use it to try and get his hand to let go. Blood is going everywhere as Katya hits him one more time, harder than ever. That does it. His eyes roll back, and his hand goes slack. I pull it off and roll away, hoping to get far enough away before he regains his senses, if he regains his senses.

Katya hits him again. Her face is twisted into a snarl. She wants him dead, very dead. She won't stop until she's sent him into the next world. She doesn't need to. He'll bleed out soon, like Vasili.

"Stop," I croak.

She looks at me, her face is very white against the BDSM gag he fitted on her.

"He'll bleed out. He's dead already," I tell her.

She steps back and tosses the paddle aside. She struggles to get the gag off. When she does, she throws it across the room and spits on the giant. It must be a Russian thing.

I've never spit on anyone. I stand, still keeping my distance. Some guys last longer than others. "Did he hurt you?" I ask.

She touches her cheek and I see it is starting to bruise.

"Shit. The fucking bastard! That's going to show," I curse. I limp over to him. He is still alive. His breathing labored and slow. Standing on my hurt leg, I kick him in the ribs. He doesn't groan or show pain. It is too late for him. His body is shutting down.

"What did you do to Vasili?" she asks.

"He's dead."

"They were going to kill us. He told me."

"Yeah, I figured as much. There might be more of them."

Her eyes widen. "You think there are more?"

"I can't tell. This place is a mess, but I saw some NEO Nazi flags and badges out there. These guys usually run in gangs."

"What will we do?"

"We'll take the truck. We'll drive out to the highway and head for that town we saw. We'll hide the truck just outside the town and walk into it. If they have a train station, we'll take the first train out, no matter where it goes."

She looks at me and there is fire and hope in her eyes. "Why don't we run away to Florida, Hunter? We can have a nice life there. There are alligators there. I've never seen alligators and I've always wanted to. I think we could have a nice life together. You like me, don't you?"

The giant is bleeding out at my feet, my ankle is killing me, I'm shit-scared more men will come into the house, and she wants us to move to Florida so she can see an alligator? I stare at her. I didn't expect this.

"You don't have to marry me or anything like that," she continues. "And if you get bored with me, I will go away. I won't be any trouble. You don't even have to support me financially. I can speak English. I'll get a job. I'm not fussy. I can be a waitress or even a cleaner. I don't mind."

"I have to get you to Detroit," I tell her. My voice is cold and robotic. It doesn't even sound like me. Inside me is a terrible pain far worse than my throbbing, red hot ankle, but I cannot stop the words from coming out of my mouth, "That's my job."

HUNTER

The light in her eyes dies out the same way the embers I poured cold water over this morning did. She nods slowly. There is sadness in her face. "All right. Let's get going, then. This place will soon stink worse than it does now."

I follow her out of the bedroom and at the door, I look back at the giant. He's totally out of it now. His heart is belting out the line of its song. That's how it goes. One moment, you're running on all cylinders, the next you're dead. And one day that will be me.

I wash my hands and face quickly. Luckily my coat is dark so the blood doesn't show. Once we're wrapped up in our coats again, we hustle out to the truck. It's still a nice bright day, if there can be a nice day in the middle of a Russian winter.

"You know how to drive this?" she asks.

"I can drive anything." And I can. The engine starts on the first try. I back out, turn around, and head for the road. "Do you have any blood on you?" I ask.

"I don't think so," she answers.

"Take a look. People notice things like that. They're going to notice your face anyway. Throw in some blood, and we'll be marked for questioning."

She starts to shake, really shake, and I know it's shock. She's reliving the giant, the gag shoved into her innocent mouth, the blood, and the fact that we murdered a man together. She will never be the same person who went into that farmhouse. She wasn't prepared for it. It's like being in combat. We're all like that the first time—unless you have no soul.

"If you're going to throw up, let me know. I'll stop, and you can do it outside."

She shakes her head.

I'm thinking she doesn't know how these things work. "I can feed you all sorts of sayings about what you experienced, but no matter what I say, it comes down to believing that you did the right thing, the only thing available to you. If he had killed me, he would have raped you so brutally you would have wished for death. It would have gone on for days, maybe weeks until one day, he goes so far, he accidentally kills you.

She is staring straight ahead, but a tear slips out of her eye and streaks down her white cheek.

The tears finish me. My hands jerk, a completely involuntary gesture, so I grip the steering wheel hard. Jesus Christ. I can't believe what's happening to me. All I want to do is pull her into my arms and console her, but I force myself to hold back. She already has way too much power over me. I stare straight ahead and keep my voice rational. "We were minding our own business. It's not like we went looking for someone to kill. They were. But they ran into some people who weren't going to be victims. Be happy that it isn't your blood all over that house. Be happy that you're alive. That's what you have to tell yourself. It's a good thing to be alive."

"Why do you care what I feel anyway? You're taking me to another monster who needs a virgin once a year. You say he raised you and you didn't know this. Have you never wondered what he does with the girls? What he will do to me?"

"Put on your seat belt," I say harshly.

"Fuck you," she spits and hugs herself in an effort to stop the shivers.

I let her work through things. The road winds, rises and falls as we head back towards the town. I would like to drive faster; there might be others. Yet, I have to make sure we get to a station, a way out. If the two thugs didn't have a lot of friends, it might be days or a week before their bodies are discovered. By that time, I want to be back in Detroit. I have now left three bodies behind me. If the local police find the bodies, Katya and I will be in deep trouble. There's no way they're going to believe some American thug, not even if the girl tells the truth.

I'm praying that when we reach the town, we not only find a train but get lucky; no one recognizes the truck and it doesn't all kick off before we get on the train. Two strangers in town. We'll be the first suspects. They'll be waiting for us on the next stop. That will be hell. I must park the car some-place where it won't be found immediately. I thank the powers that be for the cold. At least the sidewalks won't be crowded. I turn to look at Katya. "We're nearly there. You need to dry your eyes and try to look as normal as possible."

"All right," she rasps.

"I'm sorry he hit you."

She reaches out and grabs my hand. "I want to thank you. You saved my life."

"We're even," I reply. "If you hadn't hammered that giant, he would have killed me. So, we're even. You owe me nothing."

"I suppose you're right, but you could have left me and run after you…felled Vasili?"

"I couldn't leave," I force myself to say the words. "Without the package I was sent here to bring home."

She doesn't say any more, and I concentrate on negotiating the icy road. It was one thing handling the Sherpa. What I did to Vasili and Dimitri was quite something else. She's probably scared of me now, and while she should be, I would rather she not be. That's what happens when you show your true colors. Some people suddenly realize they don't know you at all.

A part of me wants to explain more, make excuses for the blood. I would like her to think well of me, but anything I say will sound like an excuse. Excuses are stupid things. Own your life—good or bad.

The town comes up faster than I expected. I slow down. I need to hide the truck.

KATYA

I cannot stop shaking. It's true that we are both alive because I found the paddle and struck that man almost to death, but that's not what scares me. What scares me is when I was hitting the giant, I was like a barbarian, wild, shameless, and full of bloodthirst. I wanted to hit him, to hurt him, to … kill him for what he did to me.

God, I hated him.

I hated him enough to beat him to death. No, that's not right, I would have hit him until he was a bloody pulp if Hunter had not stopped me and killed the giant himself. I merely managed to split open his head like a melon, but I wanted him to die. I cannot get that out of my head. I wanted him to die so bad I could feel it rushing in my blood.

At least now I know that I have it in me to fight Anakin if I have to.

I push the thought away as I search for signs along the way. If the town has a train station, it will be marked. They're always marked. The government is good about signs. They want people to ride the trains. And since half the people this far from Moscow can't read, the signs are always pictures.

I spot the sign and point to it. "Over there."

He nods and we follow the arrow, turning onto another street. We're not far. We'll be there in a few minutes. I hope there is a train. I want to get away from this town as quickly as possible. Every second here reminds me of those two ... animals. Every second reminds me of the way I wanted to kill the giant. Once we get away, I can try to forget.

A middle-aged woman walking from the opposite direction stares at us curiously.

I look her straight in the eye, but next to me I feel Hunter's unease.

In a way, I'm in control. I know the dialect. I know the people and the customs. What looks normal and what doesn't. He sticks out like a sore thumb. Without the Sherpa, he has to believe what I tell him. That may be the ticket for me to get away from him. I can lie or trick him. He won't know. I'll find a way to escape, but not here. It will have to wait till we get to Moscow. It will be crowded there, and I will have more opportunities.

Silently, I point to the sign indicating a train station and he makes the turn.

As we walk into the parking lot, I think we might be in luck. There's a train waiting, and it looks like it is heading to Moscow. Well, that's what the sign on the platform it is next to says. "The train looks like it is going to Moscow," I say. "Perhaps they will have room for two more."

Hunter looks relieved. He glances around him. "I hope so. It's up to you to get us on that train."

"Should be no problem."

We walk quickly, but we don't hurry. I lead the way through the station which isn't crowded and that's a good thing. No one stands at the ticket office, and that could be good or bad. Good if there are seats available. Bad, if the train is stuck for some reason. I possess the same anxiety as Hunter has. The longer we hang around this town, the more risk we take. The way those two men looked, I don't know if I would be able to convince the police we acted in self-defense.

The woman in the ticket office tells me we're in luck. There is a cabin we can have, and while the train doesn't go all the way to Moscow, it will connect with another train in a few hours. That train will take us all the way. Hunter hands me his credit card, but I notice it is not in his name. The woman runs it through her machine, we get the tickets, she tells us to get on the train right away as it will leave in fifteen minutes.

I thank her, and we head for the platform. The station is easy to navigate. There are signs. The American spots an ATM, and we stop long enough to get some cash. That's probably smart. We are the last to board. The official who greets us is old and reminds me of the Sherpa. He points out the way, and we move down the narrow aisle.

Our little room is in the middle of the train, and I am happy to plop down on the seat. This day has been horrific. I think that only a little while ago, I was home with my parents. I was as clean and bright as an angel. Now, after three deaths, I'm on my way to Moscow to be handed over to a monster. I feel as if my life with my parents happened many years ago. So much has happened to me that I'm not even the same person I was. I look into Hunter's face and I know I will be even more different when I disappear in Moscow.

"Good work," Hunter says. "I can hardly believe we made it."

"We're not in Moscow yet," I remind him. "And we're not out of Russia."

"I know the answer is most probably no, but have you ever been arrested?"

I shake my head. "Never."

"Ever given anyone your fingerprints?"

"No."

"Good. When they find those two goombas, they might or might not process the house. If they do, they'll find our prints. Mine are on file in America, but I don't think the Ruskis have access. If yours aren't on file anywhere, their chances of finding us are pretty small, especially since there are no witnesses. I think we'll make it. But we have to get out of this country as soon as we can."

I frown. "Do you have a passport for me?"

"Yes, I do." He yawns, as the train starts to move. He stretches out on the seats. "Wake me in an hour."

I laugh. "I'm going to be asleep like you."

"Then, I'll wake you. And we'll get something to eat."

"Yes, I'm very hungry."

Hunter closes his eyes. I watch a moment before I lie down and close my own. Fatigue washes over me. I realize I'm exhausted. The cold, the Sherpa, Dimitri and Vasili, they have all sapped my energy. I'm asleep before I can remember anything else.

When I wake, I'm alone.

For a moment, I don't quite understand where I am or what the rocking sensation is. Then I realize I'm on a train, but I'm not supposed to be alone. I sit up. Where is the American? Why am I alone? I wonder if I should look for him.

Before I can decide, the door opens, and Hunter enters. He's grinning and his arms are full. "I probably got taken to the cleaners," he says, dumping his haul onto the small table. "But they have this car with lots of stuff. I grabbed some and paid cash. They seemed happy with what I gave them."

On the table are bottles of water and soda, bags of chips and pretzels, several sandwiches, bars of chocolates, and packets of candy. My stomach rumbles at the sight of food and I am reminded that I haven't eaten in a long while.

"Help yourself," he says. "I don't know how long we have till we have to change trains, but you must be hungry."

"I am, what do you call it … er … starving," I say as I grab a bottle of water and a sandwich.

"This train is OK. Not luxury but OK." He grabs a sandwich and a soda. "I found the restrooms too. They're not far."

I will use the toilets after I eat. As I sip water, I notice that my jaw hurts from where the giant hit me. The shivering begins again, deep inside and I remind myself that the giant is dead.

We have done what we have done, and now, we must flee. Hunter lied when he said he likes our chances of escape, but I truly believe I will escape Anakin. Hunter must do what he must and I must do what I must for my parents and my sister, and my own survival too.

"When we get to Moscow," Hunter says. "We will take the first flight anywhere that gets us closer to the United States. If we have to wait in some airport, let's wait in one outside Russia."

I nod in agreement, ignoring the pain in my face as I chew. The brute of a giant hit me harder than I remember. We eat in silence because hungry people are like that. I am reminded of my home, my parents. They always ate in silence. They didn't like to talk to each other, not when they were sober, anyway.

In the toilets, I look at my face in the mirror. Hunter was right; the bruise is already showing and will show for some time. But other than that my face appears unchanged. There's nothing to tell that together with the American I have murdered someone. Maybe I'm becoming more Russian in my bones. Russians are uniformly melancholy and morose. They always expect fate to deal them a poor hand and are unsurprised when it does. When I return, I find Hunter studying his phone.

"It still doesn't work," he says. "The power is down, and my power cord is gone. We'll have to look for a new one at the next stop."

I nod. Talking makes my jaw hurt too.

He looks at me, and seems to immediately understand. He

jumps up. "I'll go get some painkillers. Your jaw must be killing you."

I stand and hold out my hand. "I want to walk."

He stares at me for a moment, then silently pulls out some cash, and hands it to me.

I head into the aisle to look for what I need. For this pain alone, the giant deserved to die. I find the car with the shop. It's small and doesn't have a lot of variety, but painkillers and digestion pills are prominently displayed. I get my pills and ask about power cords, but the shop doesn't stock them. The woman there assures me I will find them at the next station where there is a bigger shop. In her eyes, I see concern for my face, and she asks if I need help. I do need help, but she can't provide it.

Only I can help myself.

I come back to find Hunter sitting with his leg resting on the little table and his ankle exposed. I can't help gasping. He must have been in agony. It looks really bad, must be swollen to at least twice its size.

He grins at me. "Not a pretty sight, huh?"

I share the pain medication with him. I feel a tinge of sympathy for him. He has his own aches. Not only his ankle, but I can also see the bruises on his neck from the giant's grip. In fact, we are both lucky to be alive.

"We need to do a little prep," Hunter says. "In case we're stopped by the police. First, neither of us ever met or talked to those two dead guys. Second, while we knew the Sherpa, we don't know what happened to him. We fell asleep, and when we woke up, he was gone. He might have gone out for a smoke and lost his way in the snow. We don't know. We walked to that town and got on the train. Enough said. The less you say, the fewer details you provide the better it will be. Play dumb. In my case, that's not so hard."

I giggle, and that makes him smile.

"I know I'm keeping this light, but this is important. I've seen this many times. Two guys do a job, and the police haul them in for questioning. They put them in separate rooms and grill them. The police don't have enough evidence to arrest either guy, but they act like they do, and they play this little game. They tell one guy that the other guy is getting ready to confess. If the other guy confesses first, then he'll get a deal from the prosecutor. So, if you don't trust the other guy, you confess first because that gets you a better deal. You rat each other out. But the kicker is that if the guys don't confess, they'll both walk away free because there isn't any evidence. So, here's where we make a pact. If we're taken and put in separate rooms, we don't confess to anything. You have to trust me on this. If you hang tough, we'll both walk away. No one will go to prison. Got that?"

I nod. I'm not familiar with these tactics, but I know the police lie and sometimes torture criminals in order to get them to confess. My second cousin was burnt with cigarettes all over his stomach when he didn't give the right answers. In Russia, every criminal confesses sooner or later.

Hunter then adds, "I promise you I won't confess. You can believe me because in my business anyone who rats isn't going to live long. Understand?"

I nod again. Even though I should hate him and he's taking me to a monster, for some weird reason I trust him.

"Good. Now, get some sleep." Hunter lies down and closes his eyes.

I follow his example. Soon, the pills will work. I know sleep isn't far away, but I hope I won't dream of anything, definitely nothing about those two monsters lying dead in their own blood, inside their stinking house.

HUNTER

After I'm sure she is sleeping I get up quietly and lock the door. I jam my shoe under the door for good measure. If I'm going to sleep, I'm going to sleep peacefully. I don't want anyone wandering in. If someone wants to talk to us, they can knock. I settle down on my side of the car and I can't help myself, my eyes wander over to her. I watch her sleeping. Even with the bruise on her face, she looks like a Princess. I have to swallow the lump in my throat when she mumbles something that sounds like Mama in her sleep. She's so young. I think of Anakin and my hands immediately clench. I force myself to look away from her.

I turn to the scenery flashing past the window. I let it hypnotize me. I stop thinking. I have a job to do for Anakin. I repeat that line until it stuns my mind. Until there's nothing left in my head except that line.

My eyes close. Sleep is welcome.

I wake when my body notices a difference in the movement of the train. It is slowing. We're coming into a station. Across from me Katya smiles a little, I guess that a big smile hurts her jaw. I hand her the bottle of pain pills. "Is this where we change trains?" I ask.

She nods.

"Luckily, we don't have a lot." I retrieve my shoe from the door and unlock it. "Got everything?"

She nods.

I put the remaining food in my pockets. We might need it later.

She smooths her hair.

"Have any idea how long a layover we have?"

She shrugs. "The trains are almost never on time. If the train is there, fantastic. If not, you sit until it is there. We Russians are patient people."

When the train stops, we get off with most of the other passengers. We move with the crowd to another platform where the train to Moscow is actually waiting. I think that for the first time since we started this journey, luck is on our side. We will need that luck too.

We find our cabin and settle in. Once again, we're alone. That's lucky too. I hand her a bottle of water, and she smiles. I would prefer talking to her, but perhaps it's better that we don't converse in English. People would remember that detail. If the police are after us, the fewer bread crumbs we leave the better.

We find a kiosk that sells phone chargers and I buy one. Having a fully charged phone is a good thing. If I can find Wi-Fi, I'll text Anakin. I don't know if he's worried about us or not. I won't say anything about the Sherpa, or the other dead guys. I have to assume anything I put in a text will be read by people on both sides of the ocean. Thinking anything less could land us in prison.

As we pull away from the station, I look out into the dark that's arriving. This train is on a direct route to Moscow and perhaps in a day, we'll be on a plane over the Atlantic. For the first time since we left the shelter, I feel like we have a decent chance of making it.

I plug in my phone and hand her another bottle of water. Got to keep her hydrated. It's many hours and many stops until Moscow and while I'd like to talk to her, I shouldn't. Soon other people will join us and it is a good habit for us to be as inconspicuous as possible.

I look out of the window and its pitch dark now. It reminds me that Russia isn't like America. I guess much of the countryside remains unlit at night. The dark rushes past, along with anything that might capture my interest. There's something beautiful about hurtling along in the blackness.

At every stop, we pick up more passengers. The first person to invade our space is a tall, thin man with a full beard. He greets us in Russian and we nod. Neither of us speaks, and that clues in the guy. Katya moves to my side and The Beard takes her spot. If her cheek bothers him, it doesn't show. Perhaps, he thinks it's nothing more than a domestic spat or rough sex. If he had met the giant, he would know just how rough the sex was going to be.

An old woman is next to join us. She carries a huge bag that she places between her feet, as if someone is going to steal it.

She doesn't greet us, and we accord her the same respect. The Beard has fallen asleep, or he's faking it.

Two students are next and they take both sides. They're eating junk food and talking. They pay no attention to the rest of us. We don't exist.

Katya lays her head on my shoulder and goes to sleep. I stay awake. Trust is an earned thing and these people have not earned any. I look out the window into the dark.

Suddenly, I'm alone with a thought just as dark as the night outside. When I get back to Detroit, Anakin will see the bruise. I quickly gloss over the part when he finds out Katya is no longer a virgin. I pretend I'll have a chance to tell him about Dimitri and Vasili. I tell myself Anakin will get a kick out of that story as he has no love for his fellow Russians who stayed behind. The smart ones, like him, he is always fond of saying, left that shithole for America years ago.

But another part of me knows these are fairytales.

Neither Katya nor me are going to get past her loss of virginity. Both of us are doomed, and yet I am too fucked up to change the direction of my fate. I'm like that dog that is beaten and kicked and abused by its owner and yet growls at anyone who tries to stop the torture or hurt his owner. I cannot stop myself from being loyal to him.

The hours pass and a young woman joins our group. She's pretty, but nowhere close to Katya's beauty. She doesn't smile when the students try to chat with her. They're not in her class and they know it. She glances at me, then looks again. I guess I am a curiosity.

Night turns into day.

Katya and I silently eat the rest of our stash.

The old man looks longingly at our food so I offer him a packet of chips. He takes it with a big grin. The old woman then suddenly cracks a toothless smile at me and I offer her one too. She takes it and smashes the chips on her gums.

Eventually, there is an announcement and everyone gathers their things. We're coming into Moscow, the end of this leg of my journey. I let the others clamber over each other in their rush to get out. Me and Katya are going to take our time. I've missed the original flight I had, but that's fine. We simply have to get a ride to the airport. Once there, we'll figure out where to go.

The train stops. Everyone crowds the aisles. We wait until the crush passes, then we leave the train and enter the station, a large and busy place.

"I have to use the toilet," Katya says.

"Me too," I answer. I point to the big clock in the middle of the floor. "We'll meet under the clock, got that?"

Katya nods. "Under the clock."

I watch her move off before I move off myself. I'm closer than ever to getting free of this place, this country. I will be very glad when I'm on the plane.

KATYA

Hunter has made it too easy for me. I know exactly where he will be when I come out of the toilets. He will be easy to avoid. In a way, I feel sorry for him. He will return to America without me. Anakin will no doubt be mean to him, but I can't let that worry me. This is my chance to escape, to not end up in someone's harem.

And it's not like I owe Hunter anything.

Yes, he saved my life, but I saved his too. If I hadn't cracked the big brute's head open he'd be dead. We'll leave it at that.

I wish I had more money, but what I have will have to do until I can find a job. I rack my brain for someone I can contact. I know of one girl from my town who moved to Moscow. With any luck, I'll be able to find her and perhaps have a bed for a night or two.

I slip out of the toilets and quickly make my way toward the exit farthest from the clock. I don't have a lot of time. As soon as he figures out I'm not coming out of the toilet, he'll start a search. By then, it will be far too late. I'll have become part of the teeming millions of Moscow. I'll be invisible. Finding me in Sutgot was easy. Finding me in Moscow will be a nightmare. I don't look back.

But I'm not smiling as I reach the exit. I feel as if my heart has been torn out of my body. I feel as if I'm bleeding out.

HUNTER

HTTPS://WWW.YOUTUBE.COM/WATCH?
V=1W7OGIMMRC4

(Sweet Child Of Mine)

I watch her leave the toilets.

I watch her glance at the clock before she turns for the exit.

I could stop her. I should stop her. If I go back without her, Anakin will probably kill me. He doesn't accept failure. I'll make up some excuse and say she was just too smart for me. Maybe, he'll accept that. I doubt it. Even if he does, he won't trust me anymore. But the truth is things have changed. I don't want to take her to Anakin. The thought of him putting his vile hands on her makes me sick to my stomach. I don't know what happened to all those virgins and it bothers me that I've never once seen any of them.

There is a pain inside me worse than any beating Anakin has given me as I walk back to the clock to wait. I have to put on a good show. I have to wait a reasonable time before I go hunting for her. I'll send a message to Anakin, because to just show up without her would be suicide. If he tells me to keep looking for a day or two, I'll keep pretending to look.

If he tells me to come home, maybe I'll fly to Boston instead of Detroit. I can last a while in Boston or New York. Or maybe I'll just go home. I'm a pathetic piece of shit and the best thing I can do is let Anakin put me out of my misery.

People rush past as I stare into nothing. She wasn't mine. She was never mine. I could never have had her. It's better this way. My life is shit, anyway. I could never have given her what she deserved. She deserves to be treated like a Princess.

"Here you are," a voice says from behind me.

For a second I freeze. It cannot be. It just cannot be. Then I turn around slowly, my shock impossible to hide.

She pushes some kind of food into my hand wrapped up in wax paper.

"It's a blini," she adds. "It's good, very good."

I look at the blini in my hand and then at her. She smiles that beautiful, angelic smile of hers, and I just can't believe she's done this. Why did she come back? Why didn't she just keep going? I know for sure she wasn't slipping out to get some food for me. I could tell by the way she hurried that she was running away. And it's what I would have done too. Why did she come back to face a fate worse than death?

Was it for me?

I look down at the food and then back at her. No one, no one has ever done such a thing for me. Cared enough for me to put my interest before their own. I'm stunned, speechless and bewildered. She makes it seem like nothing, but it touches me. It's something a good person does. And it changes everything. Every fucking thing.

"Eat," she urges with a laugh. "Eat."

And something inside me melts. It's the jagged pieces of ice inside my heart. Suddenly, I'm warm in a way I've never been before. She gave up her freedom, maybe her life for me.

I take a bite of the blini. She's right. It's good. It's the best thing I've ever tasted in my life. Through one of the glass windows the sun shines through.

Life is beautiful. More beautiful than I ever suspected.

KATYA

I'm not one hundred percent sure why I came back. My head said I should keep on going, that it would be an utterly stupid move to go back, that I should find a new life in Moscow, but my heart, my poor, stupid, young heart wouldn't let me take one more step away from him. My heart only remembered all the white scars on his body. So many and some of them so deep. They're everywhere. On his back, on his thighs, his arms, his chest. There is even one on his penis. I could feel the thick, raised skin against my tongue when I took him into my mouth.

I know without being told that Anakin is responsible for all of them.

As a child, I was hit only once by my father, and even then he came and sat on my bed that night and apologized for losing his temper. I can't even begin to imagine what kind of childhood Hunter must have had. I feel angry for what happened and I know Anakin will hurt him badly if I run away while I'm under Hunter's care, therefore I will go with him to America, but once he has passed me over to Anakin, I will do what I did to the big brute back in the farmhouse if I have to. I will kill Anakin. I know now I'm able to kill any man who threatens my survival.

But I will never be the reason Anakin gets to hurt Hunter again. Even if he doesn't want me, he is my man and I'll protect what is mine.

Hunter looks into my eyes, and there is something different about him. It's like his eyes are shining with something, but I don't know what. I just know I feel goosebumps all over my skin. It's crazy, wild and amazing, but I dare not hope.

He has disappointed me before.

"I will make you a promise," he says in a shaking voice. "Anakin will not hurt you. I'll see to that and if he cuts off your parents, I'll make the payments."

I smile at him. "You promise?"

"I promise." He leans closer, intimately close. "I will not let anyone hurt you, not Anakin, not fucking anyone. Do you understand? I don't know how you feel about me, and I'll understand if you don't like me. It's not easy to warm to a man who has killed people, but I'll take care of you Katya. Until you tell me to stop, I'll be there for you."

I want to tell him that I more than like him. I think I might even have fallen in love with him. He kept me alive in a blizzard, saved me from being raped and killed by a beast, and he has been true to me in his fashion, but I remember how he rebuffed me when I asked him to run away with me to Florida, so I'll proceed carefully. "You will take care of me in America? I mean, until I can find a job?"

"I'll take care of you under any circumstances. And I promise that you will love America. It's the greatest country in this world or any other."

I nod. I know both of us are ignoring the elephant in the room. Anakin! And what he will do when he finds out I'm not a virgin.

Hunter lifts my chin and kisses me. Anyone watching will think we are young lovers on our way to a sun-drenched holiday or something, they don't know we are fugitives and what lies before us is a monster called Anakin. I like his kiss, it tells me what he cannot. I would like to have sex with him again, but the kiss will have to do for now.

He takes my hand and pulls me toward another exit. I go happily with him. I have given up my plan to stay in Moscow. I will go to America. I will trust. My heart will not allow me to do anything else.

Outside, we find a taxi that will take us to the airport. The taxi is dirty and cold, but I no longer care much. I'm excited about being with him. I don't care what's waiting for us in the future, as long as I'm with him. I've read great Russian literature and there's nothing in there like what I feel. The intensity of what I feel shocks me. We don't speak in the taxi, but it doesn't matter because we sit so close together I can feel the heat from his body and his hand never let's go of mine.

At the airport, he takes over again and is quickly able to secure us seats on a plane to London. I've never been on a plane before and I feel excited about it. Hunter hands me my passport. To my surprise, I find it is an American passport and though it has my photo in it, I'm identified as an American woman.

The plane leaves in an hour, which suits Hunter very well. He wants to get out of Russia as soon as he can. The connecting flight from London to Detroit is for the next day, which means we will have to spend a day and a night in London. That suits me. Even if everything goes to pot later, I will have that one night with him in a hotel room.

I will make it a special night.

HUNTER

Everything goes more smoothly than I could have hoped for. I think she must be feeling that same relief because as soon as we sit, she orders a vodka, smiles broadly and greets the woman sitting in front as if they are old friends. When the alcohol arrives, she throws it down her throat and orders another one. I love to see her so thrilled about something and it kills me to tell her to go easy. Alcohol loosens lips, and I don't want her speaking to the woman in front or anyone else about her escapades. Also, she has the wrong accent for an American woman.

While we're practically out of harm's way, we're not there yet. We do something stupid, and the police will pick us up in London. I have no illusions about what will happen then. Being an American with a police record is a recipe for disaster.

The plane backs away from the gate and taxis toward the runway. Outside, I can see snow beginning to fall. I have a sudden urge to abandon Detroit and move to Florida. It never snows in Florida, or so I've been told. And they have alligators there. We pause at the runway, and the pilot tells us that we're third in line. I'd like to be first, but third will suit just fine.

The snow can't get that bad in the next ten minutes.

It doesn't. Once we're off the ground, I breathe more easily. I'm off Russian soil, and that's a big deal. My chances of being arrested for murder have gone way down. When we land in London, I'll be even happier.

Next to me, Katya is entranced by what is happening outside the window. I can't tell if she's truly happy or a bit sad. She's leaving mother Russia, but she didn't have all that great a life as far as I can see. Still, she had to leave her family and that must be hard for any young girl.

People lie all the time. In fact, it's smart to just assume that everyone lies. That way, you won't be so disappointed when you find out they're lying. I lie. I know I lie, but I really meant what I told her. I won't let Anakin or anyone else harm a hair on her head. And if need be, as I promised, I'll take care of her parents. It's against my way of thinking, but I'll do it. I don't break promises. That's another reason she's going to Detroit.

I promised Anakin.

KATYA

Hunter wakes me just before we land in London. The sun has risen, and there are no clouds. I can see London as we approach the airport. It is massive. After all, it is one of the largest cities in the world.

Since our flight isn't for another twenty-two hours, we are going to leave the airport. To do that we must clear immigration. The agent who processes us takes our passports from us. Hunter looks cool and unaffected, but I am shaking inside. Even my mouth feels dry with nervousness. What is the punishment for travelling under false papers?

He wants to know the purpose of our trip. Hunter explains that we are on a layover. He shows them our tickets. The agent glances at our tickets then stamps Hunter's passport. He doesn't stamp mine. Instead, his eyes slide over the bruise on my cheek before he looks at my photo in the passport. I wonder if he thinks I'm being kidnapped and forced into some sort of sex-trafficking ring. I can see an implacable quality in his eyes.

I grin widely at him. "I'm so madly excited because I've never been to London before."

He doesn't smile, but he stamps my passport and ushers us along.

Hunter looks down at me. "You can start breathing again," he says, his eyes amused.

Outside the terminal, we get a taxi, and to my surprise, Hunter tells the driver to take us to Harrods. I've heard of the store, but of course, I'd never dreamed of going there.

"You can't show up in Detroit dressed like a tramp," he says. "And I could use a change of clothes too."

It's true, both of us look like tramps. How long has it been since I had a bath? Far too long. I'm sure I smell like a goat or worse. "Isn't it very expensive there, though?"

"I think I can afford it," he says easily. Then he pauses, a hard expression coming into his eyes. "Anakin is looking for a princess and I'm going to give him one. You can't look too good if you're going to fool him."

I'll never be a princess, but I can certainly look better than I do right now.

Harrods is more luxurious than anything I have ever seen. As we pass through the perfume section, a couple of beautifully dressed sales people actually raise their eyebrows and crinkle up their noses at us. Hunter doesn't even spare them a second glance. He takes me upstairs to the women's designer section where he finds a store assistant. She takes one look and smiles as if she has just won the lottery. I guess she must work on commission or something. Hunter tells her what he wants, and she promises to put it all together. A dress, a pair of jeans, some blouses, underwear, makeup and shoes. I suppose everything I will need to transform into a princess and a suitcase to put the stuff in. Hunter gives the clerk two hours to finish, and then he leaves.

"We'll start with underwear," she says. "Practical or sexy?"

"Sexy," I say automatically. "Very sexy."

She smiles. "I know exactly what you need."

The next two hours pass far faster than I expect. The clerk, whose name is Samira, puts me through a number of changes. As I'm finding the perfect wardrobe, another clerk arrives to organize my makeup. She tells me I have excellent skin and I tell her she should see my sister's skin. Then she instructs me on how to apply the makeup so my best features will shine. The way she gushes on about my features makes me feel embarrassed because she uses words like perfect, absolutely beautiful and stunning. Other sales clerks start to come in to watch.

In the end, she turns the mirror around and I have to believe her. I do look like a runway model. My cheekbones are 'perfect'.

When I turn around, Hunter is standing there holding a large shopping bag. He looks different too. He hasn't changed his clothes, but he has had a shave and his eyes are brighter. We stare at each other for what feels like forever. I know I love him with all my heart. We've been through so much I feel bonded to him. No matter what happens now, I will always, always love him. Then he smiles slowly. His smile is genuine. I hope he likes what he sees because I have changed into new jeans and top too.

I like the way I look and I think he does too.

He settles the bill and I'm sure he gives a generous tip because the clerks tell us to come back soon. It feels incredibly good to have someone wait on me. I can't believe it's happening to me, a simple village girl from the backwaters of Russia.

He leads me out to another cab that takes us and our bags to a hotel. The hotel lobby glitters with gold, mirrors, marble surfaces, and many lights. It looks like a palace to me. I can't help but smile. I've never seen anything like it in real life. This is the stuff of magazine pictures.

We breeze through the lobby where a smiling young boy takes our bags and escorts us into the elevator like we're the most important people he will see today.

Oh my, I think I could live here.

As the doors close I meet Hunter's eyes in the mirrored doors and something secret passes between us. Like a current of electricity. No one else can see it or feel it. It's just between us.

I know he doesn't feel about me the way I feel about him, but he wants my body.

The boy asks him something, but he doesn't answer, just stares at me. There's a little ding and the doors slide open smoothly. The boy takes us down a corridor. The carpet is so soft and plush and it feels as if my new shoes are sinking into it.

The boy opens the door and I'm amazed by how beautiful the suite is.

Our room is a suite with fresh flowers, a lovely green and cream living room. There's a basket of fruit and a bottle of champagne on the coffee table next to a sofa.

While Hunter talks to the boy I wander into the bedroom. It features a view of downtown London. I stare out the window and think myself very, very, very lucky. How did this happen? For that moment, I forget that I'm on my way to Anakin. I turn, and he is smiling.

"Take a bath or a shower," he says. "Then get dressed for dinner. We're going to have a great dinner."

"We can have room service. I've always wanted to order room service like they do in Hollywood movies."

"We'll use room service for dessert. I want to experience London with you. You see, I've never done this either."

"Then, we'll do it together." I move closer, wind my hands around his neck, and press my body to him. The only thing I have is my body to show him that I appreciate what he's done, what he's doing. Almost immediately, I feel him become rock hard. I feel that heat again. I remember what he did with his tongue. I lift up my head and looking into his eyes that are half-closed with lust, I kiss him. His lips are soft and delicious and I can feel myself melting. I want to tell him I love him, but he lifts his head, slaps my bottom and tells me to hurry. We only have a few hours.

I skip to the bathroom. I haven't skipped since I was a child. I must be happy.

HUNTER

Katya's happiness both elates and hurts me. I love that she is excited, but I hate that it won't last. I go to the window and look out. London is busy, very busy. If only there was a way for us to get lost here.

No.

He would find us. He would never stop until he found us and punished me for my betrayal. I'll have to kill Anakin before he kills me. Because Anakin *will* kill me. He's killed other men for less. He doesn't abide mistakes. I frown. Anakin sent me because his usual guy couldn't make it. Nobody tells Anakin they can't make it. If his usual fetcher wasn't available, it's because he's dead. When I think about it I haven't seen Anton for more than a year. As a matter of fact, the last I heard of him was when he was getting ready to go to Russia. I feel it in my gut that something happened last year, something with the virgin.

But what happened?

I need to find out. I have to find out what happened to the

girl from last year. I hate myself for not listening more closely to Anton last year. I think a moment and wonder how I can find out. It will take a phone call and I can make the call, but not now. I'd rather not know yet. I want to have a good time with Katya tonight.

I want her to have the time of her life—maybe for the last time.

When Hunter steps out of the bedroom, I'm amazed.

He's one of those men who grow on you. Sometimes when you see a good-looking guy, you think he's gorgeous, but the more you see him the more boring his looks seem to be, but with Hunter, he just becomes ever more intriguing and handsome with time. He's what Russian women refer to as the full package. I grin inwardly. In more ways than one.

He looks at me as if he can't believe his eyes, but in truth I'm as surprised by him as I am of myself. I have looked in the mirror and I know just how different I look, how sophisticated. I look nothing like the eighteen-year-old girl who left Sutgot. The makeup, the dress, my nails, and these tall shoes that I'm afraid I will fall from.

"You look terrific," he says softly.

I let my eyes wander over the crisp white shirt, the big muscles in his shoulders and arms that the beautifully cut suit cannot hide and feel something flutter in my belly. "And so do you," I murmur softly.

He holds out his arm, and I take it. "We're going down to the lounge for a drink," he says. "Then, we're going to have dinner at a wonderful restaurant the bellboy told me about. After that, we're coming back here for dessert. We could do more, but we have to fly out tomorrow and I don't want you to be sick."

"I know it will be the best night of my life."

"You're going to have many more great nights, Katya, many more." Hunter leads me out of our room. "You smell incredible, by the way."

"I sprayed perfume in the air in front of me and walked into it the way the make-up artist told me to. I hope I haven't worn too much?"

"No you haven't, but it's all good. I like you with and without the perfume," he says huskily.

We walk into the lounge and the men look at me. I've never been looked at by such sophisticated men before. The men in Sutgot stared at me, but they were oafs. They stare at all women like that. These are rich men, educated men, men with fine suits and gold jewelry.

Hunter leads us to a table in a cozy corner and a waitress comes to us immediately. Hunter tells her we will have vodka on the rocks, and she bustles away to fill our order. I look around at this beautiful lounge, at the soft lights and expensive … everything. The background piano music fits this room, these people. This is the kind of place I have read about and seen on TV. I never dreamed I would ever be in such a place. It is too much. I almost want to cry.

"Like it?" Hunter asks.

"Tell me I'm not dreaming," I say.

"You're not dreaming," he answers.

"It's really like a dream," I tell him. "Do you always go to these kinds of places?"

"Naw," he says with a laugh. "I don't hang out in places like this. I can't afford it, but I've saved for a very long time and I don't want to die without spending it." There's something bitter about his laugh.

I take his hand and squeeze it. We're the inmates on death row who get whatever they want for a last meal. I know we're condemned and death is waiting around the corner, but I feel happier than I have ever felt. Right at this moment, I no longer care about tomorrow, about Anakin, about being a virgin. I'm happy beyond all measure. This is far beyond what I have ever imagined.

The waitress returns with our drinks, and Hunter makes a toast. "To non-virgins."

I lift my glass. "To non-virgins," I echo before taking a sip. It's the best vodka I have ever tasted.

"You're the most beautiful woman in the room," Hunter tells me.

I blush. "There are many women around us who are more beautiful."

"But none like you. And none that have come through a blizzard to get here."

I frown. "We shouldn't talk about that."

"I suppose not. Let's talk about better things. Let's talk about what you always wanted to be once you stopped wanting to be a ballerina or a gymnast. What's your dream, Katya?"

I have to think for a moment. "I haven't had a dream for several years, ever since my parents told me I was to be the next virgin. I suppose I gave up my dream at that point." I lick my lips. "What do you think happened to all the other girls?"

Hunter shrugs. "I don't know, and that's the truth. I'm not trying to spin you. I am going to try and find out tomorrow though."

"I agree. I'd like to know—but not tonight. Tonight, tonight I want to be the queen."

His gaze is indulgent. "More like a Princess, but yes, you can be the queen. Tonight, you will be whatever you want to be."

I hold up my drink, and we toast again. "And you'll be whatever you want to be. Can you be my Prince?"

He smiles. "Have you ever seen Big Ben?"

"Who?"

"Not a who, a what. It's the bell in the most famous clock tower in the world."

"Can we see it?" I ask eagerly.

"We will, on our way to dinner. We'll see it and several other famous sights. You'll be Cinderella going to the ball."

"And you'll be the handsome prince. Only I have no glass slippers."

"You don't need them. You've already snagged the Prince." He gives me a wink.

HUNTER

We don't have time to be proper tourists, so we take a taxi ride all around London, past Big Ben, London Bridge, Buckingham Palace, and the Embankment. Katya holds onto my arm and stares out the window as the driver gives us the tour. It's fine, but it's not as heady as her perfume and the vodka racing through my blood. She is a princess tonight, my princess. She's everything that any prince would ever want. I want to keep that. I don't want to think about tomorrow, or the fact that I cannot promise her anything real.

We're on our way to a feast and that's all that matters.

Katya's eyes grow wide when we arrive at the restaurant and there's a liveried doorman to open the car door for us. The place is first class all the way. A snooty headwaiter shows us to our table, and a smarmy waiter recommends expensive dishes, and we bite. I don't care. Tonight nothing matters but seeing Katya's face move from fascination to joy, to wonder, to astonishment, to amazement, then back to fascination again. Tonight belongs to her. And me. Tomorrow might be my last day on this earth, so I'm gonna make this night special.

The wine we order would eat up my entire month's booze budget. It's so much, it makes Katya's eyes pop. Why not? I think, why not order something ridiculous. We're not going to do this again. It's now or never. The food is as good as the wine. The service is exactly what is expected. Some other diners regard us with something less than respect, but that doesn't matter. I'm used to that, I have a tattoo on my neck that snakes out of the collar of my shirt. The men look at Katya and lick their lips. I can't blame them really, she's the best thing on the menu tonight.

After dinner, we go back to the hotel. It's not real late, but it's late enough. We have to fly out in the morning. Katya hangs on my arm like a beautiful trinket, but she's not a trinket. She's my trinket. I feel possession flare up inside me like a beast that has broken free of his chains. Something that I have never felt before rises up inside me. She is mine. Only mine.

In our room, I ask if she wants room service dessert, and she says no. She has had enough food and drink for one night.

"What would you like?" I ask.

She blushes then she blurts out, "I want everything. Tonight, I want us to do oral sex on each other at the same time."

A vein in my neck is already throbbing as I take off my jacket, and I feel that familiar stirring that only she can bring to my body. The yearning inside me is so elemental and intense, I can feel hot pre-cum leaking out. "Go in the bedroom and get naked."

She doesn't have to be told twice. She almost dashes into the bedroom, and Katya has no idea how much I want her, how much I want her to feel everything.

I strip as I head for the bedroom. By the time I get there, she has switched off the light. The winter moon is shining through the window, it's luminance falling on her. She's already on the bed, nude, smooth as silk, her glistening little cunt taunting me. Like an alluring moon goddess she calls to me to worship her. I slip onto her altar. My hands reach out to touch her silvery curves. I can smell her arousal and it is making me feel giddy.

"What do these tattoos mean?" she asks, delicately tracing the blue ink on my chest.

"They were my way of reclaiming my body. They helped to cover some of the scars and burn marks and gave me a feeling of being in control."

"They're beautiful," she whispers.

"I hate them. I should have saved my skin for you. Your name should be on every inch of my body," I murmur, sucking her nipples into my mouth.

She shivers. God, I love it when she shivers. Her fingers find my erection, teasing it, taming it. Her touch is incredibly erotic and I can feel my heart pounding like crazy. She's a siren, a woman I cannot resist. I pull her close and kiss her, but my desire overwhelms everything else and I … devour her.

When I pull apart we're both breathing heavily. "I can't wait a second longer, Princess. Sit on my face," I pant.

Lying flat, I help to position her so she rides my face, while facing away. Her beautiful ass looks perfect and I swipe my tongue along the pink seam. Sweet nectar fills my mouth. I've been dreaming of this. Her hands wrap around my cock as her hot wet mouth stretches around the thick mushroom head.

I groan with pleasure as I pull her perfect pussy to my face to lick up and down her slit, tasting, wanting. I've been thinking of doing this all evening. I shove my tongue deeper into her, opening her a little, preparing her for my dick. But first … she's going to come on my face and I'm going to lap it all up like a fucking hound.

I lick her all over and play with her clit. She moans and I lick a little deeper, a little faster. I lap circles around her clit. Her hips move; her pussy convulses. She wants more, and I have every intention of giving it all to her.

She squeezes me even as she sucks, and I lose all control. I'm going to climax, and that will fill her mouth with my cum. I work on her clit and pussy, and I know she's right there with me. She's incredibly wet and her body shakes with need. I think all I have to do is press with my tongue, and she'll explode.

KATYA

I can barely contain myself. I want to orgasm already, and we've just begun. I think he wants to as well because his cock pulses in my hand whenever I lick the head. In the moonlight, it looks massive, and the white scar on it makes it look wicked. I let the tip of my tongue follow the scar. His cock jumps. I open my mouth wide and close it over it.

"Fuck, Katya," he growls.

I cannot take all of it, but really, I want to swallow all of it, make it mine. What I can take, I suck slowly. I taste him and whatever juices are coming out. When I feel his tongue sink into me. I start sucking him hard. That drives me wild, and I moan all over his perfect erection. And it is perfect, it must be. It is mine. I take more into my throat and that is a strange feeling. I want to gag and yet, I don't.

He moans gutturally and licks me like a starving man. I feel my body start to quake. My hips bob up and down. God, I want him so much. I know that right now, I could take him inside me like I did that first night. I suck him harder. I feel his hips move as he pushes into my mouth. I want him to come. I want to feel him grow and explode in my mouth.

I squeal as his tongue presses on a part of me that has become incredibly sensitive, but he doesn't stay. It is just a tease. I start to beg him to finish the job. It is not enough to come close. I want the beast inside me to take over.

He grips my ass with both hands and pressing his face against me, sinks his tongue into me. I feel the climax grow inside me and start to quake. Suddenly, I can no longer hold back. The beast races through me like a fire. It burns me even as I convulse. I am lost, I am lost. I can focus on nothing but the fire. Even as his cock explodes in my mouth. Heat fills my mouth. I take it even though my body focuses on what he has done to my most private parts.

It is as near to heaven as I have ever been.

HUNTER

HTTPS://WWW.YOUTUBE.COM/WATCH?
V=IKZRIWESBLA

(Perfect)

We stop, both of us gasping for breath. I never knew she'd be this sweet. We roll apart, but we stay stuck together. Neither of us wants to move. We want to lie still and savor this, because this might never happen again for us.

"Do you know that I'm not afraid? I haven't been ever since you showed up."

I look into her eyes. They are shadowed, but I know she's telling the truth.

"You are my protector," she whispers. "You are the one I have been waiting for all my life. I think it is my fate that Anakin sent you and not someone else or I would never have stood a chance."

The moonlight throws strange shadows as I turn her and she

comes into my arms. We kiss and trade the taste of each other. A growl of triumph passes my lips. It feels right that I should taste her and she should taste me. I push her down on the bed. Need throbs inside me. It has a name.

Katya. Katya.

I rake her nipple with my teeth and she cries out. I spread her legs wide so she is completely exposed to me. Her little pussy quivers. I run my middle finger down her belly and over her clit then plunge my thick, scarred, inked ugly digit into her drenched pussy.

Her little hips writhe with anticipation.

I circle her swollen clit with my thumb and her body begins to buck. "Not so fast, Princess," I growl.

I need ownership of her. I drop my weight on her trembling body, pinning her to the bed, trapping her underneath me. I want her under me forever. Lust ripples through me as I fist my cock. Then I bend my head and lap up her juices before I capture her mouth and as my slippery tongue thrusts into her mouth, I plunge deep into her tight pussy. She gasps at the intrusion, but as I continue to pump into her, mewling noises fall out of her mouth.

I forget the world outside. I forget we have a date with the devil. I forget Anakin. I forget everything. I only know I'm where I belong. Inside Katya.

A roar sounds in my head. I go over the edge. I hear her scream. She's climaxing too. I have taken her with me. It is pure bliss. I'll never let her go. She is mine now. Forever.

I whisper her name over and over again.

HUNTER

When I wake, I'm alone.

Alone is my ordinary condition, but I went to sleep with Katya in my arms. She's not here now and the bathroom door isn't closed.

Damn.

I roll out of bed and check the suite. I call her. Then I sit on the bed. No. It cannot be. I feel hollow inside. She's gone. She's left me. I nod to myself. I don't know why I'm mourning this and acting so shocked. It's not even a lost dream. It's nothing. We were just two strangers who survived a blizzard. It was my fault for falling in love.

"She's gone," I say aloud. It comes out in a broken whisper.

I drop my head in my hands. Yes, she's gone. I lift my head and look around the room. At the champagne bottle we opened. Ah, what fun we had. I licked it off her breasts.

Then I smile sadly. *It's okay, Katya. You did the right thing.* This way you're safe. I hope she has taken enough money. I go to my pocket, pull out my wallet and frown. She didn't take anything. How can she survive without money? She will get taken advantage of.

I get dressed. I have no idea how to find her, but I know I have to try. I have to give her enough money or alone and vulnerable, she will end up homeless on the streets of London. She will get raped. The thought sends me crazy. I hope the desk clerk noticed her and which way she went. I rush into my clothes and slide into my shoes. Just as I start for the door it opens.

I freeze.

Katya smiles as she enters. She's holding a paper bag from a coffee shop down the street. We saw it together last night. I remember her saying, *"That little coffee house is so pretty. Maybe we can have coffee and scones together before we leave tomorrow."*

"Coffee and scones," she announces. "I knew we wouldn't have time to visit the shop before we left this morning." She puts down the sack and comes to me.

We kiss, a short kiss.

She backs up a step. "What's the matter?" she asks. "You look as white as a ghost."

"I …" I shake my head.

"Tell me what's wrong. Did Anakin call?"

"I thought you were gone."

She jumps at me and holds on to me with her hands and her legs. "I'm not leaving my man. I had my chance in the train station, remember? I'm never leaving you," she whispers in my ear.

I don't reply.

She understands. I can't reply. If I speak, I will do what I haven't done since I was a boy. I will break down and cry. I will become weak and not do the things I have to do. For a long time, we remain like that. Then I find my voice. "Jump in the shower," I tell her. "We have to get out of here soon."

She unwraps her arms and legs and slides off me. She looks at me flirtatiously from beneath her lashes. I still remember how innocent she was that first night when she just took off her clothes and stood there without an ounce of flirtation in her. "Are you going to watch my ass as I walk to the bathroom?" she teases.

She's giving me a way out. To protect my manliness.

"Yes," I admit.

She laughs and walks away. I do watch her cute, little ass disappear. Then I send a text to Anakin:

I have the package. Catching the next flight out to Detroit.

HUNTER

https://www.youtube.com/watch?v=ScNNfyq3d_w
-Show me how to be whole again-

Katya sleeps almost all the way to Detroit. I guess the events of the past few days have sapped her energy. Katya and I have done a lot together. The blizzard, Vasili and Dimitri, shopping, dinner …We have stuffed a lot of living into our short time together. Her blanket slips and I gently pull it back over her shoulders. How things have changed. How I've changed. Once she was a package. Now she's part of me. More precious to me than my own life. I feel so protective of her that even the thought of anyone hurting a single hair on her head drives me into a blind rage.

I suppose we're like soldiers who go into battle together. No matter how the soldiers went in, they come out like brothers. Katya and I are not brother and sister … not even close, but we have bonded in a way that's impossible to break. I would kill for her. No, that I could have done anytime—I would die for her.

Instead of being tired, I'm wired. I cannot sleep.

While waiting for the flight, I managed to send an email to a buddy in Anakin's organization. Waiting for our luggage, I get the answer. It's not what I want. It's not even close. According to my bud, the reason I went to fetch Katya was because Anton, the previous fetcher died while trying to help his girl escape. In fact, they both died. It was how Anakin paid the fetcher for his unfaithfulness.

No doubt, I'm in line to enjoy the same fate.

My phone pings and it's a text from Anakin. He wants me to bring Katya to his house in the suburbs as soon as we land. Anakin has a big place there, far bigger than he needs since he has never married. I've never been invited to go there until now. As we head for long-term parking, I notice Katya looks very pale. It's as if the reality of our situation has just hit her.

When she catches my eye though, she smiles bravely.

She's the condemned prisoner waiting for the hour of reckoning. A part of me wants to cheer her up, but that part loses to the part that tells me to remain aloof. I cannot take my mind off the meeting with Anakin. There's nothing more important than that.

I must remember that.

We ride through the city and Katya looks out of the window curiously, but she doesn't say anything. I guess there's nothing much to say. Detroit is a gray, ugly place.

The electric gates to Anakin's house open and we drive through. Katya turns her head and looks at me. She doesn't say anything and neither do I. We pull into the drive and I see that her hands are shaking. We get out and I carry her suitcase to the front door.

Anakin's number one Goomba opens the door for us. He's a big guy, but he's slow. He doesn't smile, simply ushers us through the entry and down the stairs to the basement.

The basement has been decorated with all sorts of Detroit sports stuff. There are Lions football helmets, Tigers bats and jerseys. Hockey sticks from the Redwings, and basketballs are autographed by all the Pistons' players. There's a bar and several huge screens, filled with sports. One corner has been transformed into a theater with loungers and surround sound. Anakin loves sports and this place is a shrine to his passion.

Anakin is standing by a desk as we enter. He doesn't even spare me a glance just looks over Katya and nods with satisfaction. Yeah, he can see how sexy she is, even if she doesn't smile. He nods to a small man in spectacles who stands when we come in. He has the face of a self-righteous pen pusher.

"The Doc will check you out," Anakin tells Katya. "Go with him."

Katya and the doc head through a door to what must be some kind of bedroom or something. I hate the idea of that supercilious prick coming anywhere near Katya, let alone examining her, but I keep my expression neutral. There's more at stake here than my needs and wants.

"She any trouble?" Anakin asks me.

"No," I answer evenly. "But your Sherpa is dead."

He frowns. "How did that happen?"

"Heart attack. We lost the car in a blizzard and had to hike to a little house. It was too much for him."

"Hmmm, I liked him. He did good work for me over there."

I don't comment, and I don't mention Dimitri and Vasili.

"I got a call from my banker. One of my shorts came in. A percentage of that will be transferred into your account." He grins. "It'll be a fat payday for you."

"Thanks." The word sticks in my throat.

He goes to the bar and cuts himself a slice of cheese from the block there. "Hey, try this cheese. It's terrific."

With Anakin, you never say no when he offers you food. I go over, and he hands me a slice. I take a bite. It's like a lump of coal in my mouth. I chew and swallow automatically.

"Great stuff, isn't it?" Anakin says. He's in a great mood. "I got it from a guy in Wisconsin who owes me. He makes great cheese."

At that moment, the doctor and Katya return. She looks pale and nervous.

"Well, Doc," Anakin says. "What's the verdict?"

The doc shakes his head. "She's not intact."

"Sex?" Anakin asks.

"I fell on my bike when I was younger," Katya says.

"Shut up," Anakin snaps at Katya.

"Can't tell," the doctor tells Anakin. "Could be an accident, but I doubt it."

"Thanks," Anakin says.

The doctor turns and walks out.

Anakin walks up to Katya and takes her by the chin. "You're a pretty little thing," he says. "Too bad you're used goods."

He turns away from her, then suddenly whirls around and hits her with a backhand slap that sends her reeling.

Neither she nor I was expecting it.

"You think you can fool me?" he shouts angrily. His face is red and there's a white ring around his mouth. "You think you can make me look like an asshole you little whore?"

I know this face. I'm transported back to the past. I'm a kid again and big strong Anakin has found another reason to punish me. I know what's coming for Katya, but I'm unable to do a single thing. I am frozen to the spot. Not even a muscle can I move. If I move, the punishment will be greater. Years and years and years of conditioning lock every single muscle in my body.

He slaps her again, so hard the sound reverberates around the room. She stumbles, but does not cry out.

I stare in horror. My body feels like it is being ripped in half, but I don't move. I can't. There isn't a single thing I can do.

Then he punches her in the face and she collapses with a grunt.

My body starts trembling violently. *Move, Hunter, move.* But I can only watch.

Anakin drops to his knees straddling her and takes out his knife.

Yes, I recognize that knife. I know it intimately. It only carved out his name on my body. There's a tattoo of a pig covering it.

"You won't be such a pretty whore when I'm done with you," he snarls.

"Hunter!" Katya screams.

HUNTER

https://www.youtube.com/watch?v=3tmd-
ClpJxA&index=64&
(Look What You Made Do)

er voice is like the crack of the whip. Suddenly,
my muscles are free. With a roar of ancient and
new fury, I jump forward and tackle Anakin. He's
not expecting it and I send him tumbling sideways. I roll
away from him and spring to my feet even before he gets
to his.

He still has the knife and he's pissed as hell. "Oh, look at that.
The little coward has grown some horns while he was in
Russia," he mocks. "Was it you? Did you make her bleed?"

"You don't beat on women. That's weak," I answer.

"So it was you!" he screams. "You got your little prick all

worked up and ruined her, and then you had the balls to bring her to ME? I should have finished the job and cut that pathetic roll of soft meat from you when I had the chance!"

But you didn't and that was your mistake.

He lunges suddenly, but I'm ready. I dodge the knife and throw a sharp left hook at his kidney. He grunts with pain and flies past. I think he's forgotten about my hands. About the years of training he gave me. He never expected them to be used against him.

"Little fucker!" Anakin snarls. "I'm gonna cut off your nuts and your dick and make your girlfriend eat them raw." He fakes a lunge this time, trying to get me to commit, but that's amateur stuff.

I don't take the bait. There's nothing Anakin can teach me about fighting. I circle, lightly, evenly, but I know this can't last too long. The Goomba upstairs will suspect something. If he comes down and alerts everyone else, Katya and I are toast. Fortunately, the sounds from the sport screens are drowning out some of the commotion.

"Come on, you old coward," I taunt. I need him to get so angry he makes a mistake. "You don't have any trouble beating up a girl. Come and get a man."

That's his problem, always been his weak spot. He's too easily offended. His ego can't take even the slightest insult. He wades in, slashing wildly. I back away, like I'm scared. It's a boxer's ploy. You time your move before you get inside his reach. At the moment, his knife is at the end of its wide arc, I step in quick and bury a fist into his soft gut. He hasn't been exercising. That's for sure. He loses all strength for a moment and I grab his knife arm. Quick as a fox, I snap his elbow over my arm.

He screams like a stuck pig and drops the knife. He never expected this. I kick him full force in the groin, and he bends over in agony.

"Not so nice when you're on the receiving end, is it?" I growl.

A solid punch to his temple, and he hits the floor. I'm about to kick him in the head when the Goomba roars.

He must have heard Anakin's scream. I don't have much time, but I have enough to jump over the bar. As I land, I feel the Goomba's big meaty fist miss my head by an inch. I have no doubt what will happen if he hits me. I grab a thick whisky glass and throw it at him as I turn. It misses his neck and strikes him in the chest ... and does absolutely nothing.

But that split-second delay is enough.

Because Anakin always keeps a pistol under the bar in his town house and I'm guessing he has one here too. He's a creature of habit and he likes to have his weapons within reach. I know that and I think the Goomba does too, because he's lunging over the bar to get me before I can reach the gun. He almost does. His fingers grab my collar even as mine get the gun. As he jerks me back, I manage to stick the gun under my arm and pull the trigger.

The sound fills the room, but the Goomba doesn't release me. I fire a second time. He grunts. I jerk away and whirl. He faces me, two bloody holes in his chest. He's not going to live and we both know it. Yet, he won't give up. A snarl fills his face.

I fire a third time.

The Goomba's head jerks as the bullet passes into his brain. He's dead before he hits the floor.

I pant and watch for a moment. I want to make sure he's dead.

Anakin groans.

I climb over the bar.

On the floor, Anakin tries to move, but the pain in his useless arm is too great. He is whimpering and cowering like the coward he is.

Katya is sitting on her haunches over him.

I wonder what is going on until I see the knife in her hand. "Don't," I shout.

She turns to look at me, then she smiles sadly at me. Before I can do anything, she lifts both her hands and plunges the knife straight into Anakin's chest. He starts to flop and that's a bad sign. She's hit something vital. His eyes bulge and blood comes out of his mouth.

Katya backs away … perhaps awed by her own action.

I didn't want her to be the one who did it. I can tell her that this will haunt her for the rest of her life, but I think she probably knows that.

She looks at me, and her face is already showing the bruises.

I stand over him. His eyes find mine. I can see he's dying. "You betrayed me," he rasps. "You betrayed me."

I shake my head in disbelief, then I crouch over him. I lean close to his ear. "Go to hell, Anakin."

"I'll be waiting there for you," he gasps with his last breath.

I stand and go to her. I take the knife out of her hand. "I would have done it, Katya."

"I wanted to share the burden with you," she whispers.

I have seen grown men, hardened criminals who wouldn't have had the guts to do this to the great Anakin. And deep respect for Katya's incredible spirit rises in me, but with it comes sadness. There's blood on her face and I wipe it away gently. "Oh, Katya. I didn't want that for you."

"And I didn't want it for you."

I hang my head. "I'm sorry, I was so pathetic I let him hit you. I wanted to stop him, but I couldn't move. Please forgive me."

"There's nothing to forgive, my darling. You had your monsters to deal with. And you did. We're in this together. Sometimes you fall and sometimes I'll fall. We'll forgive each other and carry on."

My chest hurts. I never thought there was such goodness in the world.

"What do we do now?" she asks.

"Now, we find a way to blame a faceless robber. The doc is gone, so we have only our story to tell. I know the rest of the gang and I think I can convince them. They're not in love with Anakin."

"What about these bodies?"

"I know a service that takes care of stiffs. They'll handle the cleanup."

She frowns. "What will we do?"

"We'll walk away. There are lots of people who will want to step into Anakin's shoes and take over his turf. There will be wars, but we'll be gone. We'll be in Florida."

Her eyes widen. "We will?"

"Yeah, we will."

She throws her arms around me with joy. For the first time, I hold her as I've wanted to hold her since Sutgot. Now I have the right to do it. To tell her I love her. To offer her something: a life together, a family.

"I know you don't love me, but I love you," she whispers.

Tears run down my face. "Fuck, Katya. How many ways do I have to show you that I love you? You are everything to me. I love you with my body, my tongue, my hands, my dick. I might even have always loved you. From the moment I saw you, I wanted to make you mine, but I was a lost soul and I didn't believe I was worthy of you."

She touches my wet cheek. "You are worthy, Hunter. You are very worthy. I knew you were always meant for me. Always. But you kept pushing me away."

"I was an asshole. I know." I kiss her then, a desperate, happy, sad, lost kiss. "I couldn't see how we could make it, but I know now, we are meant to be."

She smiles, her face already swollen. "Do I look terrible?"

"No worse than me."

She laughs. "That's horrible."

Sergei, one of Anakin's security men runs into the room. He's carrying a gun. I block Katya's body and face him. "Put the gun away, Sergei. No need for loyalty to a dead man."

For a moment, he hesitates. "Are you sure?"

I nod.

He holsters his gun and walks over to Anakin's still body. He shakes his head in disbelief. The man he had feared for so long was dead. For a long while, he did nothing, then he kicked the corpse. "Good. It's about time someone stood up to the sick, twisted fuck." He walks over to me. "Come with me. I want to show you something."

As we watch, he touches a level in a shelf of books and it slides back to reveal a door. He opens it and switches on a light. White fluorescent light fills the space.

Katya and I follow him inside.

I hear Katya gasp in astonishment.

It is a torture room full of all kinds of elements of torment. Some I'm familiar with as they've been used on me, but others are a shock even to me. A tiny metal cage, bars on the ceiling with leather fasteners, the type of metal table you find in a coroner's office, surgical utensils, whips, electric saws, a sort of rocking horse with a huge wooden dildo that comes out of it every time it rocks. It would have torn the insides of a rider. My God, what he did to those poor girls. What a racket he was running. Bringing in innocent virgins from backward little villages of Russia and paying off their dirt-poor uneducated parents. No wonder he got away with it for so long. No one here even knew they existed.

Even knowing what a sadistic brute Anakin was, it's still a shock to learn he was a serial killer.

"This would have been my fate," Katya whispers.

I pull her towards me and hold her tightly. "Not any more, my darling. Not anymore."

HUNTER

(One week later)

I wake up suddenly in our little apartment in Florida. The dream is still fresh in my mind.

I got lost. My parents didn't sell me. I got lost in a funfair.

I was standing at the edge of the Ghost Ride crying when a man with shiny shoes approached me. He said he would help me find my parents. He took me by the hand and led me away.

"What is it darling?" Katya asks next to me.

I turn towards her. "My parents didn't sell me, Katya. Anakin stole me from a funfair."

She sits up. "What?"

"Somehow, I got separated from my parents. I was crying and he found me."

"Oh my God. That means they're out there somewhere, probably still hurting, still waiting and hoping you'll come back. You have to look for them."

I nod slowly. I remember a woman with the laughing blue eyes and I know I have to find her again. They must both be still alive. They have to be. I jump out of bed. I'm too excited to sleep.

"What are you doing?" Katya asks.

"I'm going to call someone I know. He's a brilliant investigator."

"At this time of the night?"

"Yeah. He never sleeps." I go into the living room and dial Tom.

"Hunter," he rasps. I can hear him lighting a cigarette. "What can I do for you?"

"I need you to find some parents who lost their son at a funfair twenty-one years ago."

"I need a bit more than that to go on. America is a big place, son."

And suddenly it comes to me. A blue-eyed woman saying, *'... and where do we live? We live in Milwaukee, Wis-con-sin.'* "Wisconsin," I say triumphantly. "In Milwaukee, Wisconsin. They lost their boy in Milwaukee. They're both Irish. The woman has blue eyes and curly dark-brown hair and the man is tall and broad. He has dark hair and brown eyes."

"Okay. I can start my search with that. If you think of anything else, give me a call."

I end the call. I walk over to the window and stare out into the night. The city lights never go off. I feel Katya's arms come around my chest and her body presses against my back. She's naked and instantly I feel my dick become stiff as a rod. She kisses my back. My heart feels as if it is being squeezed. "I need to fuck you. Are you wet?" I ask.

"Soaking," she admits. "You know how my pussy is always begging for your cock to fill her up."

I turn around and grab her by her delicious ass cheeks. I carry her to the dining table and lay her on it. Opening her sweet thighs, I roll her hips right off the table surface. Her wet pussy quivers as I sink inside her to the hilt. She stills, as she always does, when I don't prime her first. She feels as hot and tight as a damp fist around me. I wait to let her muscles get used to the stretch.

When she's ready for more, she arches her back and rocks her hips restlessly. Begging. She needs this as much as I do.

I withdraw and slam back in so brutally, she almost shoots off the table.

Bending forward, I capture her mouth and slip my tongue into it. She likes that. Likes sucking my tongue while I fuck her. While she sucks my tongue greedily I ram into her. It's a hard, frenzied fuck. My hardness filling her over and over again while those mewling noises she makes that I love so much are echoing around us. We come together. So hard — I see stars.

"Hunter …"

"Yes, my love."

"We will find them. No matter what."

I smile at her. "I hope so, my love. It's a hole in my soul."

TOM

I cross off the next name on my list. I'm half-way through and I already feel like a prick. The hope I rustle up when I first call and the disappointment they feel when it is not their son isn't for the faint-hearted. I pick up the phone and dial the next number.

A woman answers, "Hello."

"Hello. Is this Mrs. Quinn?"

"Yes."

"My name is Tom Watson and I'm a private investigator. I'm working for a man who wants to find his parents. I'm calling you because I believe you lost your son twenty-one years ago and I'm just trying to ascertain if he is your son. Would you mind answering a few questions? Nothing intrusive …"

For a couple of seconds there is no sound, just her soft breathing. "Yes, of course," she croaks.

"Did you lose your son twenty-one years ago?"

"Yes, we lost our boy twenty-one years ago." Her voice is shaky, but there's already a stirring of hope in it.

"Are you Irish?"

"Yes, yes, we are."

"Was he three years old when you lost him?"

"Yes." Her voice has dropped to a frightened whisper as if she's afraid she won't be able to answer the next question correctly.

"Did you lose your boy in a funfair?"

"Yes, we lost Sean in a funfair." The hope is in her voice is at the full-blown stage.

Unfortunately, I got this far once with a woman before we hit a blank. "Do you have curly dark brown hair and blue eyes?"

"I do," she says in a rush.

"Do you use the expression, 'stop acting the maggot'?"

At that moment, she starts sobbing.

I lean back. I found Hunter's parents. Actually, I found Sean's parents.

EPILOGUE

Katya

https://www.youtube.com/watch?v=MoHnffhBwqs&

(this one's for you)

Our hotel room faces a secluded beach, trickier to find, but once you find it, you have lots of privacy. The sand is littered with driftwood and skipping stones, and the ocean looks sparkling blue where the sun dances over the waves. It stretches farther than I can see. Russia is on the other side someplace. We sent money back home for my parents and I've offered to educate my sister here in America. My father has agreed to send her when she's a bit older.

I miss my family so much, but Sean says he will take me to Russia again. He tells me to hurry up and get pregnant fast, so we can take a grandchild to my parents.

The sun comes in through the window and warms my skin.

I'm thankful, very thankful for being here. It's sunny and it looks like no place I've ever been before. This is our little holiday. Sean, yeah, we found out his name isn't Hunter. His real name is Sean.

Hunter is just what Anakin decided to call him. We came here to meet his parents. It was the most beautiful touching thing I have ever seen. The way his mother held herself so stiffly until she laid eyes on him and then she just fell apart. Her boy. It was her baby boy all grown up. She cried and cried. I cried too. His father cried. Sean cried. All of us were crying for her. For her terrible, terrible pain.

For nearly an hour, she simply held Sean's hand while tears poured out of her eyes. No one said a word. She'd prepared a mountain of food for us. Every time I looked at her, I felt more and more sorry for her. What a poor thing. Her whole life had been ruined by Anakin. She had missed out on so much.

After lunch, I told Sean I didn't want to live in Florida anymore. I had hyped the alligators up in my mind. They weren't all that, after all. What I really wanted was to live in Milwaukee. I said I thought we could make a nice life here. He wants to start a pub. An Irish pub and Milwaukee would be perfect for that. He hugged me and told me I was a gift to him. A gift from the Gods for all the suffering he had endured. Without me, he was sure, he would have had an early grave in some dank lake.

"Like it?" Sean asks as his arms wrap around me. He automatically kneads my breast, the way I crave it.

"It's beautiful," I answer. "Thank you for bringing me here."

I can feel his erection slide along my thigh and I shiver. He wants me and despite our many couplings, I always want him. I want him in ways I never knew one could want a man.

"You're so beautiful," he says as he nuzzles my neck.

I moan.

"Wanna screw?" he asks.

I shiver with laughter. "You know, I always want to screw."

His hand slides up my skirt to my bare pussy, and he finds me wet. I keep it bare for him as much as I can because I know he likes to reach for it whenever he wants it.

"I can tell you want it," he says as he pulls me away from the window and back to the bed. Sean doesn't always want sex in the same way. He surprises me, and that is a wonderful thing. He bends me over the bed, my behind high in the air. He spanks me and I giggle. Spreading my legs wide, he swipes his tongue along my sensitive seam. I wriggle suggestively and he sucks my folds and clit into his mouth. His grip is so tight I can't move. He sucks until I climax, my juices pouring into his mouth and running down his chin.

He stands, wipes his chin, then takes his cock and rubs it along my pussy. I begin to quake inside. I almost never have just one orgasm. It's always two or three for me.

"Want it?" he asks.

"Yesssssssss, please."

He pushes his huge cock into me, and I gasp. Every time he does this, he makes me gasp. It always hurts a tiny bit, but I've never wanted anything half so much. He spanks me again and it burns. It makes me feel like a bad little girl, a very bad little girl. We have this game. Sometimes I call him

Daddy and I talk dirty to him. It turns him wild with lust when I play the dirty girl.

He starts to stroke, as I feel him slam deeper and deeper into me. He grabs my bottom and squeezes as he slides in and out. Then, he reaches around and presses on my clit.

"Oh, God," I groan, and press back onto his thrusts. I want more and more. I want him to never stop.

"If I hurt you," he begins.

"You will never hurt me. I can take it," I say. "Give it to me deep and hard. Fill my pussy with your cum."

"I'll do my best."

His best is more than good enough. He rams all the way in. I start to pant. Little screams escape me. He grabs my hair, pulls, and twists my head back. I found out last week that I actually like it when he's rough with me. It adds another dimension to our mating. I want all I can get from him.

"Make me cum. I'm sooo close."

He laughs and drives deep.

"Yesssss," I hiss. "Don't stop."

He kisses me even as he thrusts faster. I start to suck on his tongue. I love doing that. Once I came from just sucking his tongue.

I close my eyes, savoring the sensation of his tongue filling my mouth and his cock so deep inside me. Almost instantly, I start to climax. I can think of nothing after that. The waves of heat start to arrive. I can feel him letting go as well. We will come together.

Later tonight, I have a surprise for him. I can't wait to see his face when I show him the tiny little shoes. They're so tiny … they will make him cry.

The End

Want to read to the first three chapters of my WIP? Then read on. :-)

COMING SOON...

HIGHEST BIDDER

CHAPTER 1

FREYA

"Excuse me," the woman said loudly, as I turned to leave the table.

That tone usually only meant one thing. I'd messed up. With a sinking stomach, I turned back and faced her.

She was using her knife to dig around the rocket leaves and cherry tomatoes on her plate. "Didn't I *specifically* say I *didn't* want parmesan shavings on my salad?"

I showed her my apologetic face. "Oh, I'm so sorry. I'll take it back and get you another one."

"What kind of waitress are you? It was just a simple salad and you couldn't even get that right."

"I'm really sorry. I was sure I made a note of it. There could have been a mix-up in the kitchen. I'll just get another one for you. It won't be a minute, I promise."

I picked up her plate and turned away.

"Er...excuse me," she calls, her voice now not only loud, but sarcastic as well.

Keeping my expression polite and solicitous, I turned to face her.

"Shouldn't you take my husband's meal away too and put it under one of those hot lights to keep it warm."

The man opposite her spoke up for the first time. "No, it's not necessary to take my lasagna back. It looks so hot it will probably burn my mouth if I eat it right away, anyway."

She threw him a death glare before looking up to me and snapping, "Take his meal away and keep it hot."

"Yes of course. I flashed her husband an apologetic smile, picked up his plate and carried both plates back to the serving station.

"What's up?" Alfredo the Second Chef asks as I put the two plates down.

"Table twenty-one. She asked for no parmesan. It might have been my mistake. I can't remember if I wrote it down."

He glanced at table twenty-one then completely lost his cool. "It is that fucking bitch again. Every time she comes here there is always something wrong with her order." He crossed his arms across his chest, and demanded, "What about the other dish then? What's wrong with that?"

"Nothing. She just wants us to keep it hot while we make her another salad."

"What a stupid bitch," he cursed. Muttering ferociously to himself as he shoved the lasagna under the warmer, then walked away with the salad.

Taking out my pad I flipped back to the order and saw from my carbon copy that it was my fault. I didn't note it down. That was the third mistake I'd made that day. Maya, one of the other waitresses stopped next to me. "What's up. You look like someone stole your last dollar."

I winced. She had no idea how right her observation was. "I messed up table twenty-one."

"Don't worry about it. She's never happy, that one. I don't know how her husband puts up with her nonsense. I would have divorced her on the wedding day itself if I was him. He always looks so unhappy as well."

"It was my fault, Maya," I admitted. "She told me and I didn't write it down."

Maya touched my hand. "Hey, it's okay. Don't beat yourself about it. We all make mistakes."

Yeah, but three mistakes in one shift. I took a deep breath. I needed this job. I needed to concentrate. Alberto came back with the salad, his face still black with rage. "Here you go. Santini salad without its most important ingredient."

"Thanks, Alberto."

I carry the two plates back to the table. "Santini salad without parmesan and meat lasagna. Sorry again for the mix-up."

"Sorry no cure," the woman muttered under her breath, as if she was a kid in a playground.

When I came back to the serving station Maya said, "Look, I only have five tables left and the guys in table seven look like they're going to be here forever finishing that bottle of wine, so if you want to leave I don't mind taking over your two tables."

I really could do with leaving early. An hour and a half ago the university called to say my mother's check to pay for my fees had bounced. I needed to go through my mother's financial records and find out why. "Are you sure?" I asked her hopefully.

She grinned. "Sure. You've done it for me before."

"Thanks, Maya. You're a star."

She patted me on the back. "Don't worry so much. It will be all right, you'll see."

I took off my apron, grabbed my bag, and ran all the way to bus stop.

CHAPTER 2

FREYA

Twenty minutes later, I arrived at King's Road, jumped off the bus, and walked briskly towards my mother's boutique.

Martin, the bald headed and spectacled man who had been my mom's loyal assistant during her socialite days when we had lots of money had morphed into her new retail assistant. He was peering through the display window with a frown on his forehead.

"What are you doing here, Missy?" he asked as I walked into the store.

"I need to check out something that's in Mom's office," I said, and hurried towards the back of the store.

Closing the door, I almost tripped over a stack of samples in my rush to get to my mom's messy desk of receipts and letters. I sat in her swivel chair and pulled open her drawer. I was actually looking for Mom's bank statement, but as I opened the second drawers, my eyes connected with a strange document. Curiously, I picked it up, and I thought my heart had come to a stop in my chest. No, no, no. I reread it and I still couldn't believe what I was seeing.

I fished my phone from my pocket and dialed my mother. She picked up on the fifth ring. "I'm at the Food Hall for some groceries," she said cheerfully.

"Mom I'm in your office," I said to her.

"Why are you—" She froze when she realized what my statement meant. "What are you doing in my office?"

"Did you mortgage Grandma's house to open the boutique?"

For a few seconds there was silence. Then she spoke, her voice so soft I had to strain to hear.

"Yes."

I could feel the blood pounding in my ears. "But you told me that you had some savings ... that you sold off some of your jewelry."

"I did, but it wasn't near enough to get a location on King's Road."

My voice rose, even though I was trying to keep it down. "So you mortgaged off the only property we had left? That's the only home you have to live in, and it is Grandma's house. Dad never touched it even when everything was falling apart."

"Freya," she said with a heavy sigh. "I did what needed to be done. You know, there's no point opening in some dreary area. Even my own friends wouldn't dream of coming to see me if I had opened in Brixton or Peckham—"

Suddenly it was too much. The university calling me, the

238

Santini Salad woman looking at me as if I was a total idiot, and now this. My voice broke as tears rolled down my cheeks. "How could you do this without telling me, Mom? We talked about it and I told you opening a boutique at a time when everybody is shopping online is pure madness. I even offered to move in with Ella. You could have moved out to a slightly cheaper area and rented out the apartment. You could have used the difference to slowly pay off our debts. That was the safe option, but of course, you had to go and throw every penny we had left into this stupid store. And now we have no more assets left. What are we going to do if the boutique fails, Mom?"

"Freya, come home, let's talk."

"Yeah sure," I said, and disconnected the call. I took a few deep breaths and tried my very best to calm myself down. I didn't want to upset my mother even further. She was already going through so much, but I felt like I was suffocating in frustration and despair.

****

An hour later, and relatively calmer, I walked through the door of our apartment in Chelsea, which was technically no longer ours. I could hear her moving around in the kitchen. After dropping my things off in my room, I went to meet her.

"Hello darling," she chirped brightly as though we had never had the earlier conversion, as though there was absolutely nothing wrong in our lives. "I'm making dinner. I got you your favorite. Belugia caviar and I'm steaming those small potatoes you like so much so you have them together."

Whatever bit of calm I had worked so hard to claim was gone. "Mom!" I yelled.

She turned to me. "What?"

I couldn't believe her. I gazed at my forty-five year old mother and I could have sworn she was the most naive person that I had ever met. "What part of we are completely broke, don't you understand? We've defaulted on several monthly payments already. We'll be foreclosed on at any moment! You bought caviar?"

"It is your favorite and," she said, looking confused, as if she couldn't understand why I was being so unreasonable.

I couldn't hold back the agony any longer. "Yes," I screamed. "When dad was alive. When we were bloody rich, and when we weren't on the brink of being fucking homeless."

"It is only a thirty-gram tin," she muttered.

Gazing at her small frame, and bedazzled turban made me feel a strange mixture of admiration and exasperation. She refused to cower down to the lowly status my father's death had brought us to. She looked nothing like an impoverished widow. Her robe was of the finest silk, her ears glistening with diamond studs, and her house slippers were made out of some kind of special material that was imported from llama growing country.

"*Mom*," I wailed, not knowing what to say or even think. "Mom!"

I felt so sorry for her, but at the same time I felt even more sorry for myself. This past year had been a nightmare beyond compare and it seems as though we weren't done falling yet.

I wanted to break down, but I could not. It would finish us both.

So I turned around and stormed out of the kitchen.

"Freya," she came after me. "Where are you going? Freya!"

I banged the door shut, and half ran all the way to the bus top.

CHAPTER 3

FREYA

I had run out without even a coat over my jeans and jumper so when my best friend, Ella opened the door I was standing at her doorstep shivering like crazy.

Her eyes widened in shock. "What are you doing?"

"Visiting you," I said through chattering teeth.

She pulled me into the house and shut the door.

When she turned around I threw my arms around her body. Automatically her arms went around me and for a while neither of us spoke. Then she quietly asked, "What's the matter, Freya?"

When I didn't respond, she went on. "Did something happen to you mother?"

I shook my head.

She scowled. "So what happened? Why are you like this?"

I tried to hold the tears back, I did everything I could, but instead they rolled helplessly down my cheeks.

Ella didn't ask any more questions. She pulled me towards her warm living room and together, we plopped down on her couch. Then she held me in her arms, whispering again and again. "It's okay. It's okay. Whatever it is we'll work it out together."

The doorbell rang suddenly, making both of us jump. I jerked away and we stared at each other. Her hazel eyes looked almost gold in the warm light of the lamp on the single book shelf behind her. The bell rang again, this time more insistently.

I sniffed. "Are you expecting someone?"

"No."

She stood up and headed towards the door while I wiped the tears off my face and grabbed the remote to her television.

A few moments later, I heard Madeline's high-pitched voice, say, "Freya's here? Just the person I wanted to see." Seconds later she appeared in the doorway wearing a fantastically skimpy dress. "Hello, babe."

She peered at me. "Why are your eyes red?"

"Why are you dressed like that in winter?'

"Have you forgotten?" she asked airily. "I'm on a mission to find a stinkingly rich idiot."

"We're still on that project?" I asked, looking away.

"Bagging me a rich one so I don't have to lift a finger for the rest of my life? Yes we are."

"You know that was what my mom did," I commented

quietly. "Twenty-four years later, she's a struggling widow about to be homeless."

The room turned so silent I could hear the winter wind as it blew past, and footsteps of strangers passing on ground level above the basement apartment.

"Um," Madeline began, and I turned just in time to see her share a perplexed look with Ella. Ella immediately joined me on the couch. "You're about to be homeless?"

Madeline came over to sit at my feet.

"It's almost certain. Mom mortgaged the apartment to open the store six months ago."

"Noooo," Madeline gasped in horror.

"How did you find out?" Ella asked.

"The university called to say Mom's check had bounced so I went to her office this evening to look at her bank statement. While I was there I saw the mortgage documents."

"What did your mom say?"

I shrugged. "What could she say? Anyway, I am convinced she is deliberately refusing to understand what is going on. Like she is still shopping at the food hall in Harrods. And when I called her she knew I'd be pissed so she went all out and got me Beluga caviar and steamed eggs to appease me."

"Damn," Ella used a hand to hide her smile. "Your mom is adorable."

I looked at Ella in astonishment, but Madeline concurred. "Yeah, she is the best. Every-time I go to her store I walk away with something new. I've already told her I'm in the market for a new mom whenever she's tired of you."

"Well, you can have her." I replied, frustrated that both my friends could not see how bad our situation was. We were thousands and thousands of pounds in debt, and I would almost certainly have to leave university and get a full-time waitressing job, and Mom would probably have to declare bankrupt, lose her home, and maybe even move into a Council flat. It would kill her to do that.

"Why?" Madeline demanded loyally. "What did she do, I don't get it. She just tried to make you feel better. You're the one sounding highfalutin now."

"We're already broke," I said tiredly. "Why spend perhaps our entire eating budget for the month on Caviar."

"I still don't get what the problem is." Madeline argued.

Ella turned to her. "Stop being so dense. Caviar is rich people's food. Not for the broke and struggling."

"Are you joking? Caviar is not that expensive."

I stared dumbfounded at her.

Ella held her hand up to her forehead. "I think she does this purposely." After a few seconds she moved her gaze to me. "How bad is it? Are we talking repossession anytime soon."

"I don't know. I haven't looked too deeply, but I know the boutique is struggling."

The room went totally silent again until Madeline took my hand. "You'll get through this Freya," she assured me. "You'll be fine."

"That's what you all said to me when—

" I still couldn't bring myself to say it. Sometimes I could have sworn that it was all still just a dream. Some cold distant dream that I was bound to wake up from. I straightend my spine and went on. "It's been a year, and I'm still not fine. Nothing is *fine*."

"You've smiled again," Ella pointed out. "Remember we watched Sex and the City for days after to get through it all, and you asked the same question Carrie did. *Will I ever smile again.* "You have."

My smile was dark. "It was the wrong question. What I should have asked was, will I ever stop crying? Big didn't die, my father did."

Madeline rubbed my knee in calming motions, and soon I shook my head to push it all aside. "There's no point for any of this," I said. "I'll have to give up uni and get a full-time job."

"You can't give up Uni." Ella protested. "I already had to give it up and our dear princess here is barely thriving in hers. We both need you to graduate, get a good job and help us out."

"I'm not even offended," Madeline said, and rose to head into the kitchen. "I didn't sign up for this goddamn tough world."

We both turned to watch her dancing to the music in her head as she poured some of Ella's table wine into a plastic cup.

"How I wish I was that carefree." I muttered.

"She can afford the luxury," Ella replied, in a hushed tone. "She still has her parents. We both don't."

I began to stretch out on the sofa to sleep, but Ella pulled me back up. "You can't sleep. We have to figure out this home repossession thing."

"Not tonight. I can't take any more of life's bullshit today."

Madeline returned with her wine and kicked the sofa in agreement. "Get up. Let's brainstorm. We're good when we put our heads together."

"How much does your mother's apartment cost?" Ella asked.

I popped one eye open. "Why? You want to buy it from my mom?"

"Sure, let me just make sure I can pay my rent this month first."

I smiled weakly.

"No, really," she insisted, "how much did your mom borrow off the house?"

"I don't know. I was too shocked to take it all in properly. I'll look tomorrow."

Madeline looked at me sadly. "I think I'm going to cry."

"It's alright," I consoled both her and myself. "It's not a big deal, just a small hiccup. I'll get through it. I'll drop out of Uni and it'll all be fine."

That was when Ella suddenly dropped her bombshell. "I know how you can get at least fifty thousand pounds overnight."

PREORDER HIGHEST BIDDER HERE

ABOUT THE AUTHOR

Thinking of leaving a review?
Please do it here:

Can't Let Her Go

Please click on this link to receive news of my latest releases
and great giveaways.
http://bit.ly/10e9WdE

and remember
I **LOVE** hearing from readers so by all means come and say
hello at Facebook

The Man In The Mirror

A Kiss Stolen